Unspoken Words

Unspoken Words

Latoya Chandler

www.urbanbooks.net

Urban Books, LLC
300 Farmingdale Road, N.Y.-Route 109
Farmingdale, NY 11735

ISBN 13: 978-1-64556-038-8
ISBN 10: 1-64556-038-4

First Trade Paperback Printing April 2020
Printed in the United States of America

10 9 8 7 6 5 4 3 2 1

*This is a work of fiction. Any references or similarities
to actual events, real people, living or dead, or to real
locales are intended to give the novel a sense of reality.
Any similarity in other names, characters, places, and
incidents is entirely coincidental.*

Distributed by Kensington Publishing Corp.
Submit Orders to:
Customer Service
400 Hahn Road
Westminster, MD 21157-4627
Phone: 1-800-733-3000
Fax: 1-800-659-2436

Dedication

I want to dedicate this book to my mother, Michelle Raysor. No matter what she endured in life, her faith, resilience, and fight are what make her the phenomenal woman she is to me, my children, and my siblings. She's the reason I am the woman that I am today.

Acknowledgments

First and foremost, I have to thank God that I am in my right mind and remain in my right mind and can be creative in producing these books.

To my children: Preston, Jamel, Jaye, Kayla, and Kendall, my heart beats in love. I love all of you and push myself to the level that I do because of you.

Darryl, the love of my life, thank you for being who you are and loving me the way that you do. Especially for allowing me to drive you crazy. But most importantly, for always talking me off of the ledge. I love you to the moon and back.

To my mommy, Michelle Raysor, thank you for being such a great example of strength and for making me the woman that I am today.

I have to thank Kendra Reeves, my sistafriend. We started this literary journey together five years ago and have become the best of friends and pen sisters. I appreciate you for the long talks, writing challenges, and the push to be better. Thank you for being you.

Diane of Diane's Literary World, where do I begin? You have been the friend, sister, and encourager since I met you in that bookstore. I cannot thank you enough for being who you are, and I'm excited about this journey that we are on together.

N'Tyse, my agent, thank you for believing in me and for the opportunities you give me. You continue to push me to levels that I didn't know I could reach. I appreciate you and this winning team that I am honored to be a part of.

I have to thank my Region Care coworkers: Reeky, April, Ayoka, Tiffany L., Alexis, Tina, Neteva, Samantha, Terry, Dawnett, Emily, Te'Cheire, Jennifer, Jannifer, Rashme, and the rest of team RC (lol). I appreciate you so much. All of you make me feel like I am on top of the world with your excitement about my novels. I want to give a special thank-you to Towanna Atkinson for sharing and telling everyone about my books. I appreciate you so much. Tie, Johnny, Christine, aka Corn (lol), and Tiffany P., thank you for allowing me to drive you crazy with my ideas. I appreciate and love every one of you.

To my family and friends, thank you for believing in me and for all of your love and support.

PART ONE

In the Midst of It All . . .

Prologue

God, it's not supposed to be like this. I know I've made mistakes in my past, and you've forgiven me for them. But yet, I feel as if I am still paying for them, Naomi-Ruth mourned silently.

The rain spattering against the windowpane matched the tears trailing down Naomi-Ruth's face. Wishing for the calm of a peaceful night, she wanted to escape the present. She turned her thoughts inward, looking for memories that could give her peace. But tranquility could not find her.

Once inside her powder room, anxiety threatened to consume her. The area was usually transformed into the setting where she meditated and sought to reach nirvana, but now, that same space was unfamiliar and unwelcoming. Naomi-Ruth's heart was racing at an alarming rate as her stomach churned. Rubbing her sweaty palms together, she glanced in the mirror—and became blindsided by the reflection staring back at her. The image was unrecognizable and yet, so familiar. She looked as tired as she felt. Her disheveled hair, along with the dark circles beneath her blazing, golden eyes, took her by surprise.

"What happened to me? Where did I go? How did I get back here?"

Tears masked her peanut butter complexion, forcing Naomi-Ruth to reflect on everything that had transpired.

"At this point in my life, there's no reason to cry over what would've, could've, or should've happened. I have to face the music," she concluded.

Taking in a deep breath, Naomi-Ruth put down the test Dez left for her on her vanity when she diagnosed her. Hesitantly, she picked it up again and opened the box. Her heart was racing, and she was slightly nauseated. With trembling hands, she administered the test. Tears welled up in her eyes. Seconds seemed like hours as she waited. She could feel the nerves as she absentmindedly bit her nails. Unable to be still, she walked back and forth, and without notice, panic struck as the indicator changed to positive.

"N-no! H-how?" she croaked. Naomi-Ruth expected the words that slipped from her lips to be a whisper, but they resounded like a reverberation throughout her master bath.

"Ruth, are you all right? Please, unlock the door," Dexter pleaded from the other side of the door.

As Naomi-Ruth watched, her hands struggled to open the door. Dexter was already pushing his way inside. She instantly became speechless as their eyes met. Confused by how he got inside the house crossed her mind, but she brushed it off, assuming she'd left the door unlocked. Her heart was hammering painfully in her chest as her breathing went from quick to next to nothing at all. In her state of numbness, the pregnancy test dropped from her hand as she bolted past Dexter, almost knocking him off balance.

Chapter One

Let's Get Married . . .

"The essence of God has penetrated the atmosphere. Deliverance is here. If you have an infirmity, a lack, or whatever, give God the praise. Praise your way through and out. He is here. Give Him honor," Pastor Lewis encouraged the flock.

The tone of the temple changed. The blessings of the Divine Spirit had permeated the parish, and they took off in praise.

Rising to his feet, basking in the aura, Pastor Lewis made his way down the three steps that led to the podium over to Naomi-Ruth, handing the mic to her without enunciating a sound.

Promptly as her palms caressed the mic, Naomi-Ruth sang. From the depths of her heart, the song grew and swelled, and you could understand every phrase drifting from her bee-stung lips. There was a precious anointing in the temple. He is here! He is here!

For a moment, Naomi-Ruth and the crowd were one. Her trouble was their trouble, and her joy was their joy. A slow, rolling crescendo strengthened. It spread quicker, more bountiful, and louder . . . until it plunged into the hearts of those accepting, gripping them in its rhythm.

The sounds from the hymn chanted to Naomi-Ruth's hidden grief, prohibiting her from delivering another note. She used her free hand to erase the tears from

her coffee-hued eyes before returning the mic to Pastor
Lewis.

As the parishioners and Naomi-Ruth gathered themselves and took their posts, Pastor Lewis hummed.

"The Spirit has stretched through this place. The Lord
brought a great Word through an outpouring of the Holy
Spirit. Did you receive it this morning?"

"Yes, He did. God showed up and out. Amen, Pastor,"
the saints chimed in.

"I will not preach behind that, but I want to leave you
with a few scriptures. Sister Naomi-Ruth, please take the
other mic and read a few verses of scripture for me."

Acknowledging his request by nodding her head in
agreement, Naomi-Ruth made her way to the choir stand
to fetch the other mic.

"Please turn your Bibles with me to Matthew 25:10,
Luke 14:8, and Revelation 19:7, and I assure you, I won't
be before you too long."

"Matthew 25:10 says, 'And while they . . . the bride-
groom . . . to the marriage.' Luke 14:8, 'When . . . any
man to a wedding . . . thou be bidden of him,' and
Revelation19:7 '. . . wedding of the Lamb has co—'"

"Stop right there," Pastor Lewis interrupted, making
his way closer to where Naomi-Ruth sat. "What's the key
word that sticks out for you, Sister Naomi-Ruth?"

Dropping her head down to search the passages of
scriptures without realizing she was still speaking into
the microphone, Naomi-Ruth mumbled under her breath,
"Marriage or wedding. I have no idea."

As the congregation erupted in laughter, Naomi-Ruth
lifted her head and was instantly blinded by the tears
flooding her eyes. Witnessing Pastor Lewis on bended
knee in front of her with a 14-caret white gold engagement ring caught her by surprise.

Naomi-Ruth's thoughts instantly consumed her without notice. She could not believe what was taking place right before her very eyes. They'd been seeing each other for a few months now, but their relationship was nothing serious enough to hint at or merit a marriage proposal. All of their outings had been group gatherings or get-togethers. Pastor Lewis and Naomi-Ruth barely spent any time alone. If and when there was a need to be paired up on teams, they'd be sure to partner up. Other than that, they'd only shared a few innocent episodes of flirting via text messaging. Nothing had ever signaled or hinted that he was in love with her, or he wanted anything remotely close to marriage.

Pausing for a long moment, and then adding, more hesitantly, "Are you sure this is what you want, Pastor?"

"Naomi-Ruth, I am certain God handpicked and handcrafted you for me. It simply took one glimpse into your brown eyes for me to see your soul and know you were all mine. Your passion for God is infectious. My heart becomes tender, and I feel like a great king when you are near me or directly in my presence. And that pure, heavenly voice of yours shoots chills up my spine and bliss to my soul. So, to answer your question, yes, I am sure my life would be complete if you would take me into your heart and grant me the honor of becoming First Lady Lewis."

Sinking into a kneeling position in front of him, Naomi-Ruth reached for his hands. As their palms joined, her tears burst forth like a flood from a dam, pouring down her face. Like a young child, her chin quivered as she responded, "Yes, I will marry you, Pastor. Yes, I will marry you."

The observers instantly chatted.

Naomi-Ruth recognized the tears threatening to overflow from his eyes. As he cradled her in his arms, tides of tears broke loose and poured faster than his pulse.

"There isn't a dry eye in this place, but we have a wedding to get ready for," Mother Diane Lewis informed everyone through fresh tears as she broke their embrace.

"N-now . . . Now?" Naomi-Ruth's eyes expanded.

"Yes, baby. It is better to wed than to burn with passion. And from that display between the two of you, the love and affection you two have for each other are clear. No worries. We will get you together so you can make my grandson an even happier man."

With her heart pounding like a thousand drums of adrenaline surging through her frame, Naomi-Ruth followed Mother Diane and two of her assistants. Naomi-Ruth's dear friend, Desirae, walked alongside her, glaring at her in a puzzled way. Without expressing a word, their eyes talked for them. Desirae didn't agree with the impromptu marriage, as she has always felt Pastor Lewis was very controlling. However, she identified that Naomi-Ruth's dream from youth had been to marry a preacher.

"Give us a moment to run back upstairs and get things situated. Sister Desirae, please help this baby get into this dress and fix her face because she done cried herself into a raccoon," Sister Lewis directed, pointing to the soft white, off-the-shoulder, lace, floor-length wedding gown embellished with beads hanging on the door of the pastor's study.

"Take it easy, Mother Diane. You need not be doing any running," Desirae diverted.

Taking a step toward the door, gripping her walking stick, she threw over her shoulder, "I'm going to use wisdom and take the elevator up, baby."

Feeling paralyzed, Naomi-Ruth stood with a mixed expression of dazed confusion and amazement on her face.

"You don't have to do this, Nomi. If he loves you and feels you're supposed to be his wife, he can wait and do it right," Desirae snapped, facing her.

"Y-you . . . You didn't help with this?"

"I had no idea."

"But the wedding dress—"

"Yes, I will agree, the dress is gorgeous, and from the looks of it, it's a perfect fit, but I had nothing to do with this. I was blindsided right along with you."

"*Blindsided?* Yes, it was a surprise, but I wouldn't call it blindsided. You don't understand, Dez."

"What is there to understand? He proposed during the service, which was cute and typical for a pastor, but I am not knocking him. Instead of allowing you to experience the joys of planning your wedding, he thought it not robbery to have a dress picked out and wedding ceremony planned? A bit extreme, wouldn't you say?"

"Out of all of the women in the church, Dez, he chose *me*. Can't you cry, be on edge with me, or just be happy for me? He's in love with me. Why would I make him wait? I'm all right with this."

"Look, I love you like a sister, and I want what's best for you. I know you are the best thing to happen to him, but you cannot allow things to start off like this. He will end up taking you and your voice from you."

"Me and my voice? What are you saying?"

"He picked out your dress and set a wedding date in place without consulting you at all. Little girls grow up envisioning the perfect wedding, and you couldn't even take part in trying to bring part of that to reality. Not for nothing, you two weren't even dating, for God's sake. Naomi, you don't even know what he's like underneath that garb. Please don't let him turn you into a *yes-person*."

"I hear you, Dez, but the problem with most marriages in African American households is we've become too independent. Women don't know what it means to be submissive."

"Submissive and stupid are two different things."

"I don't want to do this right now, Dez. This is my wedding day, so can you please just be happy for me? Besides, this has to be ordained by God."

"I am overjoyed for your engagement, but rushing to get married the same day of your proposal is a bit much for me to swallow. Also, please, keep in mind that God isn't the author of confusion. Did you even talk to Him about this?" Raising her hand to stop Naomi-Ruth from speaking, she continued. "No, you didn't. Why? Oh, I will answer that as well. It's because you didn't have time to. You, my dear friend, got engaged, and now, you're getting married within an hour on the same day." Uncomfortable and feeling a tad bit troubled for her friend, Desirae quickly gathered her wits. "You're absolutely right, Nomi. This *is* your day. Although I may not agree with what you're about to do, let's try to make the best of it."

Much to Desirae and Naomi-Ruth's surprise, the ceremony was elegantly beautiful. It pretty much mirrored the wedding of Naomi-Ruth's dreams. Each of the pews had white tulle garlands with lighting to accentuate the white rose petals that adorned both sides of the aisle. Towering rose arches with the same tulle and lighting were erected at the beginning and end of the aisle. Desirae struggled to control the influx of tears that stormed her face as she walked hand in hand with her childhood friend down the aisle. Because Naomi-Ruth's parents were deceased and Desirae was the only living person close to family, she escorted her best friend down the aisle.

Naomi-Ruth's eyes darted around as she neared the end of the aisle. Her free hand clenched into a fist at the end of her lace sleeve, pulling the fabric nervously. With trembling lips, she whispered, "Dez, w-where . . . Where is he?"

"I-I don't—"

"*I need thee, oooh, I-I need thee . . . No matter where or how far I've searched, the love I wanted was never in reach. When you crossed my path, Love was sent to me for you to teach*," Pastor Lewis serenaded his bride as he tearfully sauntered down the path leading him directly to her.

As Desirae gripped Naomi-Ruth's hand, hesitating to release her, Pastor Lewis took his place to the right of them at the altar.

"Marriage is a blessing. Who presents Naomi-Ruth to wed this man, Pastor Dexter Lewis?" Elder Gerald Martin solicited.

"I-I do, but she gives herself with blessings from God," Desirae stuttered. Pulling her in to embrace her, she whispered, "Are you *sure* you want to do this, Nomi?"

"I'm positive." She kissed her on the cheek.

Releasing her, she stared at her bosom buddy wide-eyed and fearfully worried. Then Desirae broke down. "I love you, Nomi. No matter what, I will always be here for you." She then took a seat on the first pew.

As Mother Diane sat beside her, Desirae wept with deep-body, thrashing sobs and softly moaned with sadness. Filled with emotions, she witnessed Naomi-Ruth vow to take a man she feels her friend knows nothing about from the other side of the pulpit. While Naomi-Ruth pledged to love, honor, obey, and submit from the script written by the man she's vowing to, Desirae's body was overtaken in a fever of misery, and nausea gripped her middle as a sick feeling swept over her. Uncomfortable with the sudden emotions that seized her, she bounded from her seat and dashed toward the doors. Stopping in her tracks before exiting, she turned to face the trail of unspoken words and emotions sitting throughout the congregation.

"I-I'm so sorry, Nomi. You know I don't know how to pretend or be fake. I love you, my sister, and always will. Please remember, no matter what, I will be here for you when and if you need me."

Chapter Two

Shaky Grounds . . .

What do newlyweds do once the honeymoon is over? Still in seventh heaven, Naomi-Ruth glowed, admiring her husband from the passenger's seat as their mini honeymoon ended.

As long as she could remember, she had desired to marry a God-fearing man and live happily ever after. She had always longed for that fairy-tale wedding and honeymoon. With a pastor as her father, Naomi-Ruth's image of the perfect man mirrored her dad. In her eyes, Pastor Lewis couldn't be any closer to reflect. Everything was so surreal for her. Not only had the ceremony embodied the wedding of her dreams, but Pastor Lewis had put it and the mind-blowing honeymoon together himself. Naomi-Ruth had only traveled outside of the suburbs of Long Island once when she was a teenager. Other than that, it was for an event supporting her father or Pastor Lewis's church. Thus, she'd spent the first day of her four-day mini-moon in Lake George in tears. It had been one of the most incredible hotel experiences she'd ever had. She didn't want to leave the glamorous lobby with glittering chandeliers and gleaming marble floors. The fifteenth-floor suite they'd shared looked out on the skyline and Yara River, and the luxuries in the room were beyond what Naomi-Ruth could've imagined. To top it off, Pastor Lewis had set up a fantastic excursion of riverside horseback riding and hot-air balloon sightseeing. The romantic special flight put Naomi-Ruth in awe. The only thing she could do was sob as her groom gloated proudly. Obviously, his mission in their marriage was to keep a smile on his wife's face.

"You've made me the happiest wife in the world," Naomi-Ruth gushed.

"That's my job," Pastor Lewis returned as they made their way to the door of his captivating, three-bedroom, two-and-a-half-bathroom condo that was a well-lit oasis of tranquility.

Covering her mouth, she exhaled. "All of this for me? What did I do to deserve this?" Naomi-Ruth stood astonished, mesmerized by the dozen different assortment of flowers adorning the living room.

"I didn't know what your favorite flower was, so I got some of everything."

"You've made the dreams I didn't know I had come true," she blubbered, unable to control her breathing like a child trying to stop crying.

An introductory meeting of their lips took place, followed by an intense, irresistible melting of their flesh. Their mouths moved in unity. They devoured each other with their lips and tongues. Incapable of containing the obvious craving to become one with his spouse, Pastor Lewis lifted Naomi-Ruth off her feet and carried her into his master bedroom and bedded his wife for the first time. During their honeymoon, he decided the right moment would present itself. He felt they didn't need to rush the intimacy. Their bodies would lead them. Their hearts would know. At this hour, Pastor Lewis knew. The time presented itself for them to consummate the vows they'd sworn to each other.

***

Naomi-Ruth moved slowly, inching one leg, then the other, until they were hanging off the bed, and she could ease her way to her feet, then tiptoe from the bedroom. After making her way downstairs, momentarily, surprise captured her tongue, witnessing a now-empty living room.

"Dex . . . Dex . . ." She grabbed her chest, almost walking into Pastor Lewis.

"I didn't mean to startle you, my love. I felt you leave the bed. I'm surprised you didn't hear me behind you."

"I-I didn't hear you at all. What happened to all the flowers?"

"I cleaned all of that up for you. We are one now, so there's no need to lie dormant in yesterday. Today is a new day for us."

"Oh, Pastor Lewis, I mean, *Dexter,* you're full of surprises." She slipped her arms around his waist, laying her head on his chest. She whispered, "I cannot wait to see what you have in store for us today."

"Well, we must deal with first things first, my beautiful wife. Let me give you a tour of our home. You don't have to worry about clothes because you have a whole new wardrobe. As the pastor's wife, you have an image to uphold, so I purchased some things for you."

"Really? How did you know my size?"

"When God sends you a great thing, He leaves no stone unturned. This is your walk-in closet." He pointed to a closed door that appeared to lead to another bedroom.

Speechless, Naomi-Ruth cried tears of joy mixed with some unnerved feelings that suddenly consumed her.

"You are beautiful, Naomi-Ruth. I used to blush just looking at you. Sometimes, I had to look into the congregation so I wouldn't lose my thought. I had to focus because I'd get lost in your beauty. Now, I don't have to worry about any of that because God saved you just for *me*." He twisted her around and joined his mouth with hers.

Locking his hands with hers, he snickered, "You're irresistible, my love. I cannot imagine my life without you. I am honored to have you as my wife."

"I am speechless. Words cannot describe the emotions that have captured my entire being. You've made my wildest dreams come true."

"God knows our hearts. You know as a pastor, but a man first, I have expectations, which is why I thought it'd be best if we started fresh."

"Whatever you need, I will do and be all that you want and need me to be, my beloved."

Brushing his hand along the side of her face, he confessed, "You are my rib, and I am now complete. Not every woman could handle or is qualified to be the first lady. God created you just for me. You may not know or be aware, but I am not a fan of makeup, pants, or sneakers. You're beautiful without all that extra stuff. I also believe women are dainty and should always drape themselves in skirts, dresses, and heels."

Naomi-Ruth blinked and stared at her mate in horror. Her hands trembled as she tried to make sense of the words spilling from his lips. As her heart raced, she felt breathless, like he had knocked the wind out of her. She could not understand how or why the things she's passionate about and made a living doing were now wrong or perhaps a sin in her husband's eyes. Outside of spending her every waking moment confined in the four walls of the church, Naomi-Ruth was a highly recommended and desired personal stylist and image consultant. She helped her clients develop and enhance their professional and personal images. Naomi-Ruth selected clothing for a variety of occasions and assisted people in choosing which styles were flattering and communicating an appropriate message.

How can I not wear jeans and a blazer? There's no way I can provide a beauty boost in things that I'm unable to take part in.

With tears bucketing down her cheeks, she defended, "I have never done too much in the way of makeup or pants. I've always dressed modestly. If I am not mistaken, being who I am and how I carry myself are the things that grabbed your attention."

"Well, you now have my undivided attention. Unless you're searching further for extra attention, none of those material things are necessary."

"Dexter, I do this for a living. How will this work or make any sense to my clients?"

"That's another thing we will have to discuss. My wife needs to be full time in ministry. I can't imagine building up this ministry without you by my side at all times. In my dream, or vision, I should say, you want these things since I seek to have them. Am I incorrect? I can't be because God doesn't confuse."

Each gasp was like a searing pain rushing down her throat. Her mind was scattered, sending her thoughts in a million different directions. Naomi-Ruth didn't understand what was happening as her dream had been to work in the fashion industry and to spend the rest of her life with a preacher like her mom. What was wrong with her having both? She had never put anything or anyone before God, which caused her to be at a loss for words and completely baffled.

"My love, you look like you've seen a ghost. We don't have to talk about this now if it's too much for you all at once."

"I-I think I need a little time to digest and make sense of it all. If you don't mind, I might do better with some fresh air. My life just did a complete 180. I need a moment to try to catch up with it."

"Of course, you do. Take all the time you need to get comfortable. I will be upstairs in my study. Before I forget, I left something for you on the kitchen table." He kissed her forehead.

Naomi-Ruth turned in the opposite direction, and her eyes crinkled as she made her way into the kitchen. There, she saw a table spread of eggs, bacon, toast, pancakes, sausages, grits, biscuits, tea, coffee, apple juice, orange juice, water, and what appeared to be a love note along with a single white rose.

"Oh my! Who did he plan on feeding with all this food?" She shook her head.

"I didn't know what you liked, so I had a little of everything prepared for you." Dexter startled her again.

As her stomach turned to ice, Naomi-Ruth confessed, "You scared me again. I didn't hear you come up behind me."

"My apologies, beautiful. Please have a seat and enjoy your breakfast." He pulled her chair from the table.

"Thank you, but I don't have too much of an appetite."

"At least have a glass of juice and some eggs."

As soon as Dexter excused himself from the kitchen, Naomi-Ruth opened the love note he left for her.

To my beloved wife, Naomi-Ruth,

I, Dexter Lewis, promise to love and honor you until I take my last breath. I write this as you sleep, and as my emotions have gotten the best of me. I cannot express how much you've made my life complete. I sought God long and hard, and when He showed me you were my wife, I made sure to prepare the perfect wedding, honeymoon, and home for you. God ordained this union, and what God joined together, no man or woman can tear apart. Not everyone will agree, understand, or

approve. However, the Bible instructs man to leave fa-
ther, mother, friends, family, and foe, and in marriage,
become one. We are no longer two individuals but have
formed a new unity. With that, I think it is best you
break it easy to Desirae with the letter I have enclosed
for her as we do not welcome her in our home. She took
malicious satisfaction with that outburst on one of the
most important days of our lives. I cannot tell her where
to worship. However, she won't be a suitable fit for
where God is taking us. She will bring us down.

I love you, Naomi-Ruth. This will be hard, but there's
nothing too hard for God.

P. S. I have an exciting day planned for us and left
your outfit for the day on the bed for you, my love.

Love always,
Your king and pastor,
Dexter Lewis

With trembling hands, Naomi-Ruth closed the letter
and sobbed.

God, I would never question you because I know your
ways aren't our ways . . . But why? I thought this would
be one of the happiest times of my life. Yet, I feel as if my
world has just come tumbling down. I've put no one or
anything before you, God, so again I ask . . . Why?

Chapter Three

The Pain of Being Different . . .

Pastor Dexter Lewis was born to Anastasia Lewis, who was 12 at the time. A parishioner at the church Anastasia and her foster family attended had raped her at the age of 11 and impregnated her during service in the church restroom. Her foster parents didn't believe in abortion as they considered it a sin. Therefore, they forced her to carry and birth her rapist's son. At 12, Anastasia struggled to give birth for three days and died during delivery because of severe bleeding. As a result, Diane and her husband, Reginald Lewis, adopted Dexter into their family of seven. Diane struggled with conceiving because of premature menopause as her menstrual cycle ceased when she was 26.

Reginald and Diane, like so many others, stood at the altar, envisioning their beautiful lives together. As the years tumbled by, Diane begrudgingly threw away many negative pregnancy tests. They dreamed of having a son to carry on the family name. No matter how hard they tried or followed instructions, it was impossible. Considering she was medically unable to conceive and being a product of foster care herself, Diane opted for becoming a foster parent. Although disappointed with the outcome, Reginald had wanted to do whatever he could to make her happy. He'd been aware of how adamant Diane was about displaced children and preventing them from becoming products of the system.

They longed for a son. However, God blessed them with daughters—five to be exact—Ramona, Taniece, Chanté, Anastasia, and Alethea. When Anastasia passed, the Lewises took Dexter in and adopted him as their son-slash-grandson. Although they adopted Dexter, they opted to call him their grandson as Diane didn't feel like she had any right or place to call him her son. Internally, she felt Anastasia's passing was her fault, and she could have prevented everything that had taken place.

Dexter grew up in somewhat of a middle-class family. All of his physical needs were met. He'd eaten three healthy meals a day, had clean clothes, and a clean house to live in. On the surface, they appeared to be a "normal" family, but behind closed doors, things were different. Being the youngest and only boy, Dexter became the family's "CinderFella."

Diane and Reginald spent most of their time in the church house. Therefore, they often left Dexter in the care of his older—and evil—foster sisters. The sisters blamed him for the death of Anastasia. They knew Dexter had been brought into the world forcefully, and, as a result, in their eyes, Anastasia died because of him, which left a hole in their sisterhood. The girls' bond had been clannish, and outsiders had not been welcome. Back then, if you hurt, betrayed, or disagreed with one—you felt the wrath of *all* of them.

At 12, they inducted Dexter into the role of CinderFella. Ramona, the oldest of the four sisters, had been the closest to Anastasia and knew how much it pained her to carry and birth a child of the man who stole her innocence. Dexter became a constant reminder of the agony her sister underwent for a year before passing away from complications of childbirth.

"Ramona, why didn't you tell Dexter, Happy Birthday?"

"What's happy about it, Taniece? Our sister passed away giving birth to him."

"I know, and it hurts like hell, but we have to be strong, Ramona."

"I'm trying to, but that doesn't mean my feelings can and will change. Our sister is gone, but he lives. There's nothing to celebrate. He should've died, not Anastasia." She broke down.

"We have to try to not think like that." She sniffled before continuing. *"You know G-ma Dye is going to check you if you don't acknowledge her precious jewel."*

"I don't care. Why do we have to cook and bake a cake for that little fag anyway?"

"Ramona!"

"What?" She rolled her eyes.

"Tolerate him like we've been doing while they're around. If we don't look after him, they will make us go to church every second."

"I'll try, but I can't stand that little boy."

With that, Dexter's childhood became a living hell. While the Lewises were out of the house or sight, the girls forced him to operate in his newfound CinderFella role. They treated him as if he were their maid between talking down to him and making fun of him.

"Clean that bathroom," one sister said.

"When you finish, get to them dishes," the other said.

"And don't drag your feet," they ordered daily.

Dexter spent many hours in his room, hiding and envisioning a different life. The schoolkids and his evil sisters bullied him regularly. The kids made fun of him and called him everything *except* Dexter. When it occurred the first time, he came home from school and cried to the girls.

Rolling her eyes and taking in a deep, aggravated breath, Ramona mocked, "What's wrong with you now? What's the baby crying about now?"

"The . . . the . . . The kids at school keep calling me names. They said my clothes are old-fashioned, and I'm a sissy."

"That's terrible, but I have something for you to wear to school tomorrow. We'll show them who's the sissy. Go take those clothes off. I'll be right back."

"Thank you, Ramona," he sniffled.

"Here, put this on," Ramona smirked, reentering the room and handing Dexter a hot pink training bra, black skirt, and Momma Dee's blond, pixie-cut wig.

"I'm not a girl," he fussed, shoving Ramona's hand.

"Oh yes, you are! Now, put this on and get to cleaning, little Miss CinderFella."

Dexter sobbed as he draped himself in humiliation.

"Keep crying, and I'm going to give you something to cry about," Ramona threatened.

After many gruesome months of being tortured by his foster sisters, Dexter took an interest in any and everything his G-ma Dye had going on. He did whatever he could to avoid being left alone with his foster sisters, especially Ramona. Without fail, no matter how old they were, they took pleasure in making his life a living hell. It seemed as if the older they got, the worse they were.

Dexter ended up spending so much time with G-ma Dye at church that he didn't pay attention to the fact that his foster sisters moved out and found a place of their own. They came for Sunday dinner faithfully and sometimes during the week, depending on their financial situations at those times. However, it was nothing like living under the same roof with them. When they came by, Diane and Reginald would be home, interfering with their light torment of Dexter until it subsided.

***

The more time Dexter spent in church, the more curious he became about the things being ministered and taking place. He wanted to know more about this God who kept Diane and Reginald out of the house more than they were at home and had parishioners passing out in church, crying, and flipping out of their shoes and wigs. All of this was difficult for Dexter to believe and comprehend. He didn't understand how everyone had these experiences they were talking about. They were worshiping and celebrating someone they've never seen. Dexter became enthralled with seeing what would happen next each time he attended a church service, so much so that he carried a pen and notebooks to take notes of the actions and reactions that took place.

At the age of 14, Dexter sprouted up, wise beyond his years. He hung on to and dissected every word that emerged from the speaker of the hour's mouth. For instance, if the pastor said something to the congregation or an individual, and it caused an aftereffect, Dexter wrote down the word, scripture, or message that prompted the response and studied it. No matter how much he analyzed things, however, it became even more difficult for him to digest the dynamics of such forces propelling people to respond in such theatrical manners. Thus, it prompted him to pinpoint the exact formula that produced such mind-blowing results.

Because of Dexter's spirit of inquiry, he obsessively searched the scriptures in-depth, seeking answers. He scrutinized the passages of scripture to the point that he became captivated with all things godlike, divine, and heavenly. While other 14-year-old boys busied themselves with video games, goofing around, and girls, Dexter read, wrote, and devoured his sixty-six books of positive direction and prescriptions. His fixation

---

consumed him so much that he could not concentrate or focus in school, which caused him to fall behind in class due to either reading his Bible while in class or skipping school.

"Dexter, come in here right now!" G-ma Dye roared.

As anxiety curdled his stomach, Dexter made his way to the front room. He had practiced repeatedly in the mirror what he'd say to G-ma Dye this weekend. However, from the tone of her voice, he could tell she had made it to the mailbox before he got to it today. Dexter had made sure to beat her to the mailbox every day to retrieve the absentee notifications.

Trying to keep his knees from buckling under the weight of his wobbly body, Dexter entered, tripping over his words, "Y-yes, G-ma D-dye."

"How are you missing days and failing when you go to school every day and spend countless hours studying and doing homework before and after school in the library?"

"G-ma Dye, the Bible says in everything we do we must put God fir—"

"What does that have to do with you missing school and failing your classes?"

"I never planned to miss school. I went to the library before school to read, and I ended up getting lost in my studies. I lost track of time."

"What are you studying if you're failing everything connected to the school, Dexter? Better yet, how in God's name are you able to spend all of that time in the library without someone calling the school?"

"No one paid me any attention for a while . . . until a couple of weeks ago. Then one clerk asked me questions at the library over by the school, so I took the bus to the one across town, and it was as if no one knew I was there."

"They ought to be ashamed of themselves—"

"I apologize, G-ma. I know I should be in school, but it's just so hard to explain. In the beginning, I was going to church with you just to get away from Ramona and the other girls. Then every time I saw how the pastor or speakers talked, their words made people cry, scream, or fall out on the floor. In the beginning, I thought it was some circus routine because it seemed so unreal to me. But the more I went, the more it made me want to understand what was happening and how it happened. So, I began to study every movement and word. I still don't know how it happened, but what I know is the more I read, the more specific things became clear to me. G-ma, right now, I think God is calling me, and school is getting in the way."

"Lord, have mercy, Dye. The boy has found the Lord," Reginald interjected.

Mumbling incoherently through her hands, Diane choked on her sobs.

No longer speaking as a teenager, but as an adult, Dexter's voice poured out like a river. "Why are you crying, G-ma? I thought if anyone could understand what was happening to me, you could. I could feel it bubbling over in the pit of my stomach. The Lord put a strong word in my heart. Upon waking and going to bed, the Bible is heavily on my mind. I even dreamed about me preaching before people. I didn't ask for this, G-ma Dye. I began studying as a joke to mimic everyone, but something caught hold of me."

Through constant sniffles as if she were resisting tears, Diane babbled, "I-I've prayed for this, baby. All I want is for you to know God for yourself and not for the God I know and taught you to know, baby. I-I didn't think it'd happen to you now at this age, honey. My heart is overjoyed."

***

The very next day, Diane made arrangements to have Dexter homeschooled. They spent at least three to four hours a day studying the Bible.

It had gotten to the point that Dexter could go to the Bible, pull a text, prepare, and memorize a ten-minute sermon. At 16, their senior pastor appointed Dexter youth pastor of New Life Christian Center. At this tender age, he based his motto on his stern belief that life is no fluke of nature. God does nothing accidentally, and He never made mistakes. Dexter not only appealed to the youth but the elderly as well. His keen eye for details manifested in the elaborate vision attracting the young, the old, and nonbelievers.

Chapter Four

The Battle Within . . .

Years of trying to uphold a high standard and being placed on a pedestal, unlike other girls your age, can take a toll on you. Naomi-Ruth was born into this, and it's been with her forever. She was and will always be the daughter of a preacher. There wasn't any way around it. The fact of the matter is she was born to Reverend Levi and First Lady Vera Patterson. Although she entered the world an only child, like every other PK, Naomi-Ruth shared her dad and mom with the church. Everyone in the congregation was her brother and sister, forcing Naomi-Ruth to live in a glass bubble doubled with high expectations.

Naomi-Ruth had been a real good preacher's daughter . . . until she turned 16 and let it all loose. Then she became a hell-raiser. She wasn't mean and vengeful, but any time she could misbehave, she did. Naomi-Ruth looked forward to communion Sunday because she sneaked out of Sunday school and into the kitchen and drank the communion juice.

Growing up with an unwavering foundation in and around the Bible, Naomi-Ruth lived by her father's teachings. God is our protector, and He will not allow any harm to come near her or her dwelling. At least, that had been her interpretation of the scripture. This text, in particular, was one of the first scriptures she learned as it was what her parents fashioned their lives after. However, all of that changed, and Naomi-Ruth began to second-guess things when she became a sophomore in high school.

"Nomi, do you think your parents will allow you to join the basketball team if you make it?"

"I hope so, Dez. I believe as long as I stay on top of my studies, and it doesn't interfere too much with the church, they shouldn't have a problem."

Unable to hide the sarcastic-filled smirk on her face, Dez shot back, "You must have forgotten that your dad knows nothing outside of that church, so he'll think it's a sin."

"That's a good one, but you're wrong. Dad was accepted to a division-one school and—"

"What? You never told me that one before."

"You never listen, Dez. Where do you think I got this ball handle and crossover from?" She dribbled the ball between her legs.

"Me." Desirae took the ball from her.

"You wish, don't you? But Dad turned it down because he said God called him into ministry."

"He could have preached on the court if he were that good. Do you know how hard it is to get into a D-1 school? My brother has been trying for years."

Knocking the ball out of her hand, Naomi-Ruth clowned, "And it will be decades or forever because Raymond sucks."

"Whatever. You better talk to your parents tonight because the coach is posting second cuts tomorrow."

After releasing a sigh, Naomi-Ruth mumbled, "I'm on it."

"Good. Now, let's head home. I'm starving."

"I have to meet Mr. Wesley to take that test I missed. Just go, greedy. I'll do my usual swing by before going home when I finish."

***

Opening her locker, Naomi-Ruth could hear what sounded like footsteps coming toward her. Knowing she had entered the locker room alone, her pulse speeded up. "It's nothing," she told herself. "Yeah, I'm imaging things." Then her eyes darted back and forth as the floorboard groaned.

Freezing, all of her breath was trapped in her throat after realizing she was not alone and that someone was in the locker room with her. Naomi-Ruth whipped her head around as a cry broke from her lips. "Stop playing, Dez. Is that you?"

Nothing and no one responded. Her pulse roared, and fear flashed through her as a hand muffled her mouth from behind.

Before Naomi-Ruth could process what was happening, she was thrown to the floor. Instantly, she became paralyzed with fear as her gym shorts and panties were torn from her flesh.

"What took you so long?"

"Nothing."

"Nomi, look at me. What's wrong with you? Why do you look like that?"

"N-nothing . . . No reason . . ."

"Why are you crying? You're scaring me. Please, talk to me. What happened to you?"

Dropping to her knees, Naomi-Ruth bent forward on the floor, pressing her palms to the carpet. She began to cry with the force of a person vomiting on all fours.

Kneeling beside her, Desirae pressed through her tears. "Nomi, whatever it is, we can talk about it. You're scaring me. Do you want me to call your parents?"

"No. Please don't. It's my fault. I should have listened to my parents. But, no, I didn't want constant teasing, so I sneaked and wore your pants to school. Now, I'm being punished by God for disobeying my parents."

Naomi-Ruth's parents were firm believers that women were to adorn themselves in dresses and skirts because pants were for men. Women were dainty and could not be daintily dressed like a man. God created man to be the head and lead, and unless a woman was unsure of herself and her role, she should never concern herself with things of a man. In translation . . . A man and a man alone wears pants.

"What are you saying? Punish for what? God won't punish you for wearing pants, Nomi. You're scaring me," she sniffled.

Her voice cracked as her eyes burned with tears. "All I could hear was his heavy breathing and the smell of the cologne he wore. I prayed over and over, staring at the ceiling, trying not to feel his violation. He pushed himself inside of me repeatedly, Dez. I could feel my insides rip," she wailed.

"What are you saying, Nomi? Who did this to you?"

"I-I don't know. I couldn't see his face. T-The lights went out, so it was dark when he came up from behind me."

"We need to call your parents. I'll go get my mom."

"No. Please don't. This is my fault. I should never have disobeyed them. I'll be fine."

"Stop saying that. God doesn't punish like that. He's a God of love, not rape, Nomi."

She bawled harder. "He punished me, Dez. God wasn't supposed to let any harm come near me or my dwelling. But I didn't honor my parents. I sinned, Dez. I sinned." She grew hysterical.

"That's so far from the truth. I refuse to believe that. Please stop thinking like that, Nomi."

"It's true, Dez. Just promise you won't say anything to anyone. I-I'll have to make something up. I can't tell them. Promise me you won't tell anyone, Dez. Please, promise me."

After Naomi-Ruth's painful wardrobe change back into the skirt she left home wearing that morning, she and Desirae made their way to Naomi-Ruth's house. The deafening silence they shared on their way over was so thick they could carve it with a knife. Although Desirae struggled with keeping Naomi-Ruth's secret, she honored her wishes. She even went as far as cosigning the story Naomi-Ruth planned to tell her parents.

Their bond was so strong and tight-knit that upon meeting each other, they swore allegiance to each other that neither dared to violate. Naomi-Ruth and Desirae had lived next door to each other since they were 2 years old. Desirae was from the neighborhood, and her mother didn't attend church. Whenever Desirae attended service, it was always in the church van with Naomi-Ruth, her parents, and a few other kids from the neighborhood. As far as they could remember, Naomi-Ruth and Desirae had been inseparable. They did everything together, and since Desirae's mom was a single parent who worked more than she was home, Desirae spent most of her youth with the Pattersons.

Naomi-Ruth bit her lip and became interested in the strokes of chocolate-brown tones of the tiger-wood flooring in the foyer once inside the house.

"Naomi-Ruth, what spirit you done brought with you up in my house?" her mother greeted her.

"I-I had to rush home after school, and some girls jumped Nomi on her way home for no reason," Desirae said, bursting into tears.

Naomi-Ruth stood motionless. She didn't understand how God could allow this to happen, even while blaming herself for disobeying her parents. She believed what the Bible said about no harm coming near her, yet God allowed her most sacred possession to be taken from her.

"H-How could this have happened, Mama? Why would God do this to me?" Her lips trembled.

Tilting her head like a confused dog, Vera seized Naomi-Ruth by the wrist, pulling her against her. She snuggled her in her warmth and whispered in her ear, "Baby, God didn't do this. He loves you just like we do. God doesn't cause harm. He protects—"

"He protects, Mama? Protects? Where was my protection then? You do so much for your God and that church, and look how He repaid you. He didn't think twice about protecting your daughter. Some protect—"

Rage boiled through Vera's body so violently that she barely had a chance to think about her actions. The only thought running through her head was preventing any further blasphemy escaping from Naomi-Ruth's lips. Without a moment's hesitation, Vera drew her hand back, making sure the slap she delivered would sting when it landed on her daughter's face. The unexpected pain buckled her knees, bringing her down. The sound of skin-to-skin contact reverberated around the room.

"I hate you and your God!"

"Please, stop, Mrs. Patterson. She's already hurt. She didn't mean any of it," Desirae begged.

Unable to control the rage consuming her, Vera blacked out for a moment, leaping toward Naomi-Ruth. She slid her hands around her throat as the child's eyes widened in surprise.

"Vera, what are you doing? Turn her loose. The devil is a liar. He will not run rampant in my house. Leave right now," Levi rebuked, opening the front door.

Snapping out of it, Vera regained her composure and sobbed. "Levi, I don't know what's gotten into me. I am so sorry. Naomi-Ruth was cursing our Heavenly Father, and I lost my—"

After jumping to her feet, Naomi-Ruth charged past him, throwing over her shoulder, "She slapped and choked me, Dad! *That's* what she did. I was hurt at school, and just like your God didn't protect me then, He didn't protect me from your wife either. I hate all of you! You're so caught up in that church you forgot how to be my parents."

"Nomi, *please,* stop! Come back here," Desirae pleaded.

Pushing her arms back and forth, Desirae jetted behind Naomi-Ruth as a car came from out of nowhere—slamming into her best friend.

Chapter Five

I Hate My Life . . .

After suffering scalp lacerations, contusions, and a concussion, Naomi-Ruth spent a few days hospitalized. While there, she was left mostly alone with her thoughts. Her parents accompanied her to the hospital. However, after praying and learning that Naomi-Ruth wasn't in any grave danger, they made their way home.

"What do you do when death seems more attractive than trying to go on another day? How can God treat me this way? Why does He ignore my cries? God doesn't love me. How can He when He ignores my prayers, and I begged for that man to stop it? If God didn't care, why will anyone else? If I were no longer here, no one would have to worry or bother with me," Naomi-Ruth asked herself in her darkest hours of contemplating suicide.

Naomi Ruth left the hospital enveloped by a wall of pain and feeling betrayed by her parents and God. Not only had God not protected her, but her parents hadn't bothered to visit her while she was in the hospital. They busied themselves with the church and sent the church missionaries to visit with her, causing Naomi-Ruth to deepen her resentment toward them and living. As she waited for her ride from the hospital, her thoughts consumed her. Scurrying around the room, Naomi-Ruth grabbed the linen from the bed and began to tie it in knots as tears masked her face.

"Nomi, what are you doing?" Desirae snatched the noose from her grip upon entrance.

"They give everything to Him, and He still betrayed me. My parents were never my parents because they're too busy being His slaves. I don't want to live anymore. I hate this life they gave and left for me to live in alone."

"Mom, please come in here. Something's wrong with Nomi. She's talking crazy. Mom, we have to help her."

Collapsing to her knees, Naomi-Ruth reclined into a sitting position and pulled her knees into her chest. Cradling her legs, she rocked back and forth as loud sobs bolted from her lips.

"Oh no, baby, what's wrong? Please, calm down, baby. What happened to her, Dez?" Her mother's eyes darted back and forth between the girls. "Everything will be all right. Please, stop crying, Nomi." She released her own set of waterworks as the three sat in an embrace.

On the way home, silence took the car hostage. Words were nowhere to be found. Tears communicated and released hidden pain, worry, guilt, confusion, and disappointment. Rosalind wasn't a big churchgoer like the Pattersons or even like her daughter, Dez. However, she could discern there was so much more to the tears and pain in Naomi-Ruth's eyes. It was a pain that she was familiar with—and it frightened her.

Rosalind took her eyes off the road for a moment reaching for her phone, and the car swerved.

"Mom!"

"I-I'm sorry. Girls, are you all right?"

"We-we're fine," Desirae mumbled.

"Grab my phone for me, please, and call over to Nomi's house. Put it on speaker."

"Praise the Lord," Pastor Patterson answered on the first ring.

"Good afternoon, Pastor. I picked up Naomi-Ruth, and if it's all right with you, I'd like her to join Dez and me for dinner."

"That won't be necessary. Vera has dinner prepared, and Ruth has service to attend this evening."

"I-I plan on coming to Bible study tonight and wouldn't mind bringing the girls with me if that's fine with you."

"To God be the glory. It looks like we will have a full house tonight. See you at 7:30." He disconnected the call.

"Mom, since when did you start going to church when it's not a holiday and for an evening service?" Desirae's eyes stretched.

"Tonight."

Dinner was unusually silent. Rosalind tried to make small talk, but it all fell on deaf ears. After excusing the girls from the table, Rosalind called for Desirae to come back downstairs.

"Yes, Mom?"

"Sit down for a minute. I want you to be honest with me, Dez. Can you do that for me?"

"Yes, Mom. What is it?"

"Did something happen to Nomi?"

"Y-you . . . you . . . know she was jumped . . . jumped and then hit by the car, Mom."

"Yes, I recognize that. Did something *else* happen to her? She was in a dark place at the hospital, Dez. Please, be honest with me."

"Mrs. Patterson choked her," she detracted from the truth.

"What do you mean she choked her? So, she never got jumped? Her *mother* hit her?"

"No, she got hurt at school . . . I mean on her way home. She said some things about God to Mrs. Patterson, and she lost it. Mrs. Patterson said she felt bad about putting her hands on her, but Nomi saw red and ran out of the house."

"Why didn't you tell me this before, Dez?"

"I was trying not to think about that day. I feel like it was my fault. If I had just waited for her, none of this would have happened."

"Come here." She brushed the side of Desirae's face once she was in arm's reach. "My gut is telling me there is something you're not saying to me, but I need you to know and understand nothing that took place was yours or Nomi's fault. There are cruel people in this world. It isn't either of your faults that people act how they do. They must answer to God for their actions."

"I hope so, Mom. Nomi didn't deserve any of this stuff."

"I know, baby." She squeezed her.

Chapter Six

We Fall Down . . .

    Being a teen pastor hasn't been easy on Dexter or for some of the parishioners. Some feel it was too soon, and Dexter hadn't had enough experience with life. In more ways than one, many expressed their feelings to Dexter. He overlooked all the naysayers except for things Reginald revealed to him while in the car or while home alone. Reginald was nothing like G-ma Diane. He was a strict and harsh disciplinarian. He saw Dexter as the teenager he was, one who didn't respect or acknowledge him as being the head of their household.

    "Thank you for giving me a ride home, Deacon . . ." He cut himself short after noticing the icy glare staring back at him. "I mean, Pop Reg," he corrected.

    "You can cut the act, Little D. No one's around. Come back to earth, little man."

    "There is no act, Pop-Pop. I'm doing what God wants me to do. This is what God created me to do. I'm walking in my calling."

    "You may be walking into a wall. You need to read Corinthians 3:18 because you're no good to yourself at this rate. You will crash. You can't stay up that high in a cloud day in and day out. It's no good for you. You're too young."

    "I enjoy the life I chose to—"

"Boy, you sound like a robot. Do you hear yourself? Dye should have left you in school, so you could experience life and mess up like most kids your age do. No one is perfect except for God. Most teenagers abandon the church after they graduate from high school."

"So, what you're saying is you want me to abandon God and turn my back on Him to prove that I'm real and that this isn't an act?"

"Why would I tell you to do something like that? I'm not trying to get struck down by God. You need to loosen up and live a little. You're a walking, talking audible Bible. The elders in the church aren't as deep as you pretend to be."

"Pop-Pop Reg, this isn't an act. This is who I am."

"Little boy, you don't even know who you are. You've fashioned yourself around the God that Dye knows. You don't know God for yourself. You're one of the first ones to minister and say it's personal and that we all need to have a personal relationship with God, but do you even know what that means?"

"Yes, I do."

"No, you don't, but in due time, you will find out. We always do."

Once at their place of residence, Dexter stormed through the door without acknowledging G-ma Dye upon entering.

"Dexter, you don't see me standing here? That's not of God or the love of God. Where are your manners?"

"Let him have his tantrum, Dye. It's good for him. That boy's boxer-panties are up in a bunch. He needs to get them out of his tail."

"What you done said to him now, Reginald?"

"The truth. You have him walking around in a spiritual blindfold. He's too young to start like this. He's going to fall hard. You'll see."

"Reggie, why would you say such a thing? He's walking in his calling, God—"

"Is it your calling or his, Dye?"

"Reggie, the boy has a calling on his life. We sit in the same services. Better yet, you bear witness to how he carries himself here on a day-to-day basis. You know only God can keep a child his age, especially the way Dexter's kept."

"You two keep drinking from that same Kool-Aid and see what happens. I wish nothing on the boy, but his head is too far in heaven that he can't see what's in front or around him right here on God's green earth."

"Maybe it wouldn't be a bad thing for you to join him, Reggie. You're making it out to be a bad thing, and I don't see the problem."

"I know I'm not perfect, which is why I live a balanced and stress-free life. I don't walk around trying to be something I'm not or someone everyone thinks I should be. God loves old Reginald just the way he is."

"I never said God didn't love you, Reggie. You're taking everything I said out of context."

"Dye, even the Bible says, don't be so heavenly minded that you're no earthly good. I keep telling that boy the same thing time and time again. But you both will see. Just mark my words. He just finished preaching about Job, and if God allowed Satan to come for him, you and that boy better strap on the whole armor of God and have all of the angels from heaven above in attendance because the devil is coming for that boy. The Word is a two-edged sword. Mark my words, Dye."

"Life and death are in words, Reggie. Watch what you say. Forgive me for saying this, but just because you've been no earthly good and got away with it, you have no right to speak ill against that boy or punish him for your—"

"God forgave me, Dye. I naïvely thought you did too. You walk around preaching about God's forgiveness, and once He forgives, your sins are in the depths of the sea. It looks like you done gone fishing or deep-sea diving, Dye, because here I am being drenched with the words of the things that God and I thought you forgave me for."

"I . . . I—"

"Save it, Dye. Better yet, talk to God about it. You seem to be able to talk to and respect Him. Maybe He'll show you how to forgive and talk to your husband."

"I . . . I'm sorry. I—"

"I know you are. You know what? You . . ."

The talking ceased, and silence entered the room as Reginald shook his head with a look of disgust on his face. As Diane attempted to speak again, a squeal from the door cut her sentence short as the front door shut behind him.

Like clockwork as if Pop-Pop Reg had a contract with the devil himself, temptation raised its intriguing head. Feeling hurt and abused with his heart torn into a million pieces, Dexter did what he knew best. He excused himself from the not-so-welcoming dinner table and found his way to the altar of the church. Although G-ma Diane was present for dinner physically, her mind, spirit, and mental presence were wherever Pop-Pop Reg was. He hadn't returned since leaving earlier.

As the words of "I Need Your Glory" by Earnest Pugh serenaded him, Dexter kneeled before the altar with his arms outstretched and petitioned his Heavenly Father.

"Dear God, I need you now. I'm lost and confused. Your servant wants to be right in your eyes. I don't want the words of man to alter my emotions. I come to you as

humbly as I know how and ask that you guard my heart. Help me not to allow the words of man—Pop Reg's words—to take me to a low place. I put my hope and trust in you, dear God, and yet, my soul is in despair. Lord, I dwell on the things that are honest, pure, and of good report, and my soul is still downcast. I need you, Heavenly Father . . ."

The volume of music decreased.

"I-I . . . I apologize for disturbing you, Pastor Dee."

Tamariane walked toward the front of the church.

"N-no . . . No problem at all, Tamariane. Is everything all right?" He rose to his feet.

"Yes . . . Well, no. I didn't know where to go. So I just came here early before choir rehearsal."

"Have a seat. Do you want to talk about it?"

"From the time I was born, my family pretty much had me in church. You know, sort of just like you. Sunday school, youth church, choir rehearsal, prayer, and tarry service—I was there. I hope I don't sound crazy, Pastor Dee, but maybe you will or won't understand, but believe it or not, sometimes being the good little Christian girl isn't always as easy as it seems."

Nodding his head in agreement, Dexter remained attentive, allowing Tamariane to divulge her pain.

"Every day, I was told I lived a sheltered life, and I'm called Little Ms. Perfect. I am far from perfect. I have thoughts that I shouldn't have. I get angry. I don't want to come to church all the time. Sometimes, I want to stay home and do nothing except read a book or something, and that is wrong. If it isn't biblically related, I'm prohibited from reading it. Mom took all the books I borrowed from the library back because she said secular books were harmful and were not edifying for me. No good will come from reading them. She said she would not allow me to become like Jezebel and stray from God."

"Jezebel? If you don't mind me asking, what books were they?"

"*Are You There God? It's me, Margaret* and *Harry Potter*."

"I'm not familiar with either of those books. Honestly, the only book I've ever read is the Bible and books related to the Bible."

"Yeah, I know. Mom throws you in my face all the time. Sometimes, I dislike you because of it." Red leaked into her cheeks as she nervously smiled and bit her lip.

"You dislike me, Tamariane? I'm crushed."

"Wow, you make jokes, Pastor Dee. You *are* normal."

"Sometimes, I wonder if I am. Pop Reg thinks it's all an act. He doesn't believe in me. I think just like you, G-ma Diane throws me around so much that my Pop-Pop dislikes me," he huffed in a slight sulk.

"I'm sorry, Pastor Dee. I-I never stay upset with you. I am very . . . you know—"

"No, I don't. You're very what?"

"Well, I know it's wrong, and I'm sure you hear this all the time from all the girls." She took a deep breath before continuing. "I'm attracted to you. You're very handsome." She hid her face in her hands.

Dexter was blown away by her confession. A lone tear threatened to fall. He has had no one other than G-ma Diane tell him he was handsome. In the early part of his 16-year-old life, he had been called everything *except* Dexter from the mouths of his sisters.

"I . . . I'm sorry for making you feel uncomfortable. I should not have said that. I have respect for you. I know that was wrong. Please forgive me. Maybe we should pray? I'll leave, I—"

Placing his hand on her shoulder, he confessed, "Thank you, Tamariane. I don't think anyone has ever said that to me before. G-ma says it because I'm her baby boy, but

no other human being has ever said that to me. I know
God made me in His image and my handsomeness, so to
speak, comes from my inner self as that is of great worth
in God's sight."

"Well, from over here by me, I think from the inside
out, you can say it has drawn me to you, but not in a bad
way, though, Pastor Dee. It's in the most respectful way.
Maybe we should pray. I will probably get struck down
from heaven sitting in the church saying this to you.
Please forgive me."

"It's okay. I needed to hear it. I came in here feeling
downcast in my spirit, so maybe I'm supposed to hear it.
Thank you."

"You think so?" She moved closer to him, introducing
her lips to his.

Dexter jumped away from her, his heart racing.

"I'm sorry, Tamariane. I didn't mean to lead you on. I'll
leave now. Please tell Sister Kepnes I had to leave, and
she should take over for me with choir rehearsal." He
dashed toward the church doors.

Running behind him, she pleaded, "I apologize, Pastor
Dee. I *am* Jezebel, just like Momma said. First, it was the
books, and now, this. I am so sorry." Her hands shook.

Turning in her direction, Dexter addressed her. "You
are not a Jezebel. Neither the books nor a kiss makes
you a Jezebel. Remember, no matter what, God forgives.
Maybe we should pray. Do you mind if we pray?"

"Sure, but I don't want to do it here. I don't want people
coming in getting the wrong idea, you know? Especially if
Momma walks in."

"Sure thing. We can go downstairs to my study."

Once in his office, Dexter prayed for forgiveness. The
more he talked, the more he could sense Tamariane

wanting to kiss him. As she motioned toward Dexter, he opened his eyes, and instead of preventing anything from happening, he pulled her closer. Falling into the evils of temptation and against everything he's ever preached or believed in, Dexter lost his virginity in the church's basement . . . the same place where he had found God.

Chapter Seven

Lord, I'm Sorry . . .

Charging through the door, Dexter ran straight into Pop Reg.

"Boy, what has gotten into you? The Lord has given you eyes to see more than the pages in the Bible. Watch where you're going before you hurt someone or yourself."

Disregarding Pop-Pop and anything that escaped from his lips, Dexter continued his race up the stairs.

"You don't hear me talking to you, boy? That Bible instructs you to obey your parents, not just preach it."

"Go ahead and make fun of me. That's all you ever do. Because of you, I messed up. It's *your* fault. *You* sent her to me."

"Dye, the devil and all his people done has got into this boy, and he done lost his mind. Come get him before I put my hands on him."

"What are you two shouting about? I hope y'all are in here praising God with all of this hollerin'."

"If he yells at me one more time, he will be calling on God, and it won't be praiseworthy."

"Dexter, baby, is there something wrong? Look at me, child. What's the matter?"

"I-I messed up bad, G-ma. I'm no good. I let God and everyone down. How could I have been so foolish? I cannot step foot back into that church."

"You're talking crazy now. You missed choir rehearsal. It's all right. It's not a sin."

"Why, Pop-Pop? Why did you do that to me? Are you happy now? I'm not perfect, just like you said. I fell right into your trap just like you said I would." His lip quivered.

"Boy, what in God's name are you babbling about?"

"Tamariane! You *know* what I'm talking about. *You* sent her to me. *You* set me up."

"No, you preached her to you. You said, '*We emerge when we learn what God is teaching*.' You even went on to say Job became more humble and compassionate because of what he went through. I believe your topic was 'You Have to Go Through to Get Through.'" He snickered. "Now, touch your neighbor and tell them 'though He slays me, yet will I trust Him.'" He dug in.

"That's enough, Reggie. Why would you taunt him? You see, he's hurting and ashamed. What happened, baby?"

"I sinned, G-ma. I sinned right on the floor of the church. I'm a disgrace. I can never return to church ever again. I'm a hypocrite." He dropped to his knees.

"What are you trying to say? You are not a hypocrite. We all fall short of the glory of God, Dexter. You know this. God forgives. Now, please, tell me what you are trying to say, baby."

"He told you already, Dye. It sounds like the boy done fell on top of little Miss Tamariane."

"What? He did *not* say that, Reggie. Dex . . ." She kneeled beside Dexter and cradled him.

Diane's words lodged in her throat as she witnessed the display of tears and emotions emerging from him.

"There you go, Dye. The spiritual blindfold has fallen from both of you. Welcome to the *real* world."

"There's a time and a place for everything, Reginald. Be serious sometimes. Now is *not* the time for your antics."

"Oh, trust me. I'm as serious as they come. I warned both of you time and time again. That was too much pressure you all put on that boy. He's not strong enough to fight temptation. Dexter barely knows who he is, so how can he fight against himself?"

"God is his strength. He was never fighting against himself. He was fighting to resist temptation," she blubbered.

"He's been fighting with his thoughts long before this. I don't care what you say. Sex starts way before the act, Dye. You can keep climbing in that bubble all you want, trying to avoid everything. Just like puppet boy over there crying his heart out, your bubble will burst too. Well, in actuality, it just did. I might say a lot, and, yeah, it may come off harsh, but it's the truth. Now, both of you get yourselves off of that floor. God forgives, and you have to forgive yourself, Dex. It's fine to want to serve God and walk in His likeness, but for heaven's sake, don't forget to be a kid, son."

No matter what Pop Reg or G-ma Dye said at that minute, their words spilled on deaf ears. Dexter's heart was breaking into a million parts. Once in his bedroom, his thoughts lashed him. Each memory that crossed his mind provoked him to screech as if he were being struck. "What have I done?" he grumbled.

"Dex, we can pray about it. Just please open the door," Dye pleaded.

"I-I can never pray again. I prayed myself on top of . . ." His words lodged in his throat.

"That's not true. Don't think like that, baby. We serve a forgiving God."

The more Dye talked, the worse Dexter felt. He'd chosen to never return to the house of God. Nothing made sense to him any longer. Dexter's mind tormented him. He couldn't figure out how he could go from faithfully following God with everything in him to breaking His precepts in the same place where he learned of his love for God. The sanctuary was the last place Dexter wanted to be. Facing his leaders terrified him. Primarily, he feared Bishop Livingston, the God-fearing father figure who had proposed ordaining Dexter as a youth pastor. He was Tamarian's grandfather. He believed everybody would find out because G-ma Dye didn't make a move or a decision without confiding in Bishop Livingston first. He was her spiritual counselor. The thought alone made Dexter's abdomen contract, causing him to vomit.

Dexter spent the balance of the weekend in his bedroom. He refused to deal with anyone. G-ma Dye had turned into a nervous mess because he didn't talk or eat. She took trays of food to him, but every time she did, he said nothing. Just like Dexter knew she would, Dye confided in Bishop Livingston when her efforts to get him to eat or communicate with her went unanswered. Although Bishop was disappointed in both his grandchild and son in the faith, he was familiar with allowing temptation to get the best of you.

In Bishop's early years of ministry, he too had fallen victim to lust. He and his wife, Santosha, fornicated. They then become teenage parents after their first time having intercourse. Similar to Dexter, Bishop Livingston lost his virginity in the house of the Lord. However, Bishop's sin became church news when one of the busybody members caught him in the middle of the act while in his father's study. Learning of Dexter's broken state caused Bishop to circle back to the years of shame and pain that he'd pressed down in his soul.

Bishop Livingston felt powerless to evade the sympathy that expanded in his chest, thinking of Dexter's mental state. Dropping all he had been working on, he rushed to Dexter's aid. Bishop could sense Dexter's trouble in Dye's tone.

Before Bishop could attempt to knock on the door, Dye yanked it open. Her face was swollen with despair, and her voice was packed with heartbreak. She blurted, "I . . . I didn't call for you to come flying over here. That wasn't my intention at all."

"Love covers all, my dear sister, Dye. You don't have to seek me for me to show the love of God nor the love I have for this family, especially Dexter. He is the son Santosha and I never had."

Dye's words couldn't locate her. Hearing and feeling the sincere love Bishop produced provoked her to break down like a newborn.

"God's hand is all over this, Dye," Bishop reassured as he made his way upstairs.

Bishop Livingston's knuckles rapped on the door. Dexter remained balled up on the floor in a fetal position because he recognized who it was at his door. Any time Bishop came by, he had the same pattern of three sharp knocks and a pause. Every hit shot a jolt through Dexter, causing his stomach to twist.

"Son, are you really going to continue to have your Bishop stand on the other side of this door?"

Bishop's words fell on deaf ears.

"Dex, we can work this out. Please, open this door so we can talk. I recognize what you're dealing with. I've been in this same embarrassing place you're battling right now. We can pull through this together. We serve a forgiving God."

Unable to stand the hammering any longer, Dexter rose on unsteady legs, forcing his way across the room. All he required was to stop the noise so he could try to calm his brain. With shaking hands, Dexter cracked the door. His body was behind it and hardly gave up enough room to peep out. Bishop put his hand on the somewhat ajar door and prayed. Dexter granted him entrance. His heart raced as he opened it to allow entry.

As Bishop neared Dexter, the young pastor's legs turned against him, and he crumpled into Bishop's arms.

"I am here, son. I am right here with you."

"I . . . I can't go back to the church, Bishop. I let God, you, and the entire church down. I'm a phony. I can't be excused. It was in God's house." He broke their embrace.

"Child, we all fall shy of the greatness of God. And He consistently provides a way of escape. He is a forgiving God."

"He won't forgive me. I have engaged in an unjust act."

"David was a man after God's own heart. He too made a mistake, and the Bible says that God forgave him. We serve the same God that forgave King David. Just like He has forgiven David, He has forgiven you. I am standing here now in front of you on God's pardon, along with His grace and unmerited forgiveness. I've made the same mistake and have been forgiven as well."

"You have, Bishop?" His eyes widened.

"Yes, son, your bishop is no angel. The first lady and I fell into our encounter of temptation right inside of my father's study. Three months after that, we find out she was pregnant, and they directed us to wed to be right in the eyes of the Lord."

"You have a kid, Bishop? I don't recall hearing or seeing a child of yours. Only Tamariane's mom, but I thought she was a foster kid."

"Yes, she is. First Lady miscarried going into her fourth month. It shattered me greatly because the sin had caused her not to be capable of having our child. God doesn't make mistakes, son. He isn't the author of confusion, which is why you and my grandchild will seek the congregation for forgiveness on Sunday. Following that, you two will wed and become one. God will get the glory out of this. The devil is a liar."

The remainder of the week and the weekend sailed by. Before Dexter could dissect all that Bishop had spoken, along with what was going to take place, Sunday was already staring at him. Fear dominated Dexter's entire being. Standing in the face of the flock, acknowledging what he identified as a degraded sin, repulsed him, which turned getting dressed into his Sunday attire into an unfit task. Dexter felt uncomfortable putting on his suit and clergy collar. His inner critic deemed him unsuitable to represent all he's experienced God to be. Unable to clothe himself, Dexter felt it was a signal for him not to attend service. As he swept his clothing onto the floor, three intense taps startled him. Hearing Bishop at his bedroom door provoked a surge of tears to mask his face. Dexter became overpowered with emotions. Bishop hadn't overlooked him and didn't allow him to deal with the repercussions of his sin alone.

"Son, open up this door. Even if I have to dress you myself, we are going to make the devil out the liar that he is."

"Bishop, I can't do this."

He opened the door. "You can, and you will. Recognize that we are all sinners who've fallen and gotten back up. You will get back up again, but first, you have to face this head-on."

Bishop's words soothed Dexter's soul, and although he struggled, he dressed and made his way to the church house, cleaving to Bishop's arm. As they entered the sanctuary, Grammy Award–winning songstress Bettina's voice spanned the temple, filling it with the anointing of the Holy Spirit, which sent Dexter to his knees. With each of the song's lyrics, Dexter's tears redoubled. He couldn't make it down the aisle. Bowing before his Heavenly Father, Dexter surrendered and prayed for forgiveness. The more Dexter put himself at the grace of the Lord, his invocation pushed Bettina to sing straight to his situation. The melody from the phrases, *"Lord, you forgave me as though it has never taken place. You absolved me; you gave me a second chance. Just like the children of Israel, I keep finding myself at the altar of your mercy,"* made Dexter whimper, praying in passion. His petition became infectious, leading the parishioners to grab hold and take part in kneeling before God where they stood. They cried out in humility, discharging the things heavy on their hearts and minds.

As the Spirit of mercy penetrated the church, Bishop Livingston took the mic over to Dexter and whispered in his ear. "Son, let the Lord have His way."

Dexter felt like the burden of his guilt and shame had been removed. He rose to his feet, feeling lighter, and drew in the air around him, and appealed to the crowd.

"Saints and friends, this morning, I appear before you in humility, asking for your forgiveness. Some of you might already know, and if you do not, I have fallen short of the glory of God. Actually, I've messed up and sinned before the Lord. If I have offended anybody because of my actions, I apologize and beg for your forgiveness." He broke down.

Bishop removed the mic from Dexter's hand, pulled him into an embrace, and said, "Son, God and your church family love and forgive you. We serve a forgiving God, saints. Who are we to act like we haven't engaged in sin? No matter how big or small, sin is a sin. Whether it is of omission or commission, my dear people, it is a sin. Right now, we will make things right in the eyes of the Lord and continue showing this young man the love of God. Tamariane, please, come and join us."

Tamariane, feeling embarrassed and disgraced, sobbed her way over to where her grandfather and future husband stood. Within ten minutes of standing in complete unease, and at 16 years of age, Bishop changed gears and joined Dexter and Tamariane as husband and wife. Neither of them agreed with what Bishop had asked of them. However, they felt he knew better than they did. Dexter considered taking this step would put them, especially him, right before the Lord.

Three months following their nuptials, Tamariane learned that she was with child. Dexter took the news as a sign that they had made the right decision in becoming man and wife because now, their child wouldn't be born in sin. Because they were teenagers, Dexter and Tamariane were prohibited from living together or seeing each other without adult supervision. However, Dexter promised to be by his pregnant bride's side every step of the way. He said just as God has taken care of him and has been there for him, he will do the same for his child.

After becoming man and wife, nothing changed between Dexter and Tamariane. They saw each other while at church. Neither of their parents supported them in seeing each other outside of service. They talked on the phone when no one was around, but that's the extent of their communication. Bishop Livingston explained to them God would present to them when the time was right for them to spend time and get to know each other on a different level. Presently, they were extremely inexperienced to recognize or understand this information.

The entire seven months of Tamariane's pregnancy, Dexter was left behind in the dark. Tamariane didn't say much when they did speak other than say the baby was great. She devoted more time to chat about the difficulties of her pregnancy, like how much weight she'd picked up, her fear that she'd be fat for the rest of her life, and how embarrassed she was when people stared at her. Despite not being able to be active and attend the doctor's appointments during her pregnancy, Dexter felt a part of it. He recorded the days on his calendar, anticipating each doctor's visit that she informed him of and the delivery date of his son. Tamariane broke the news to him when she was six months, and she gave him some of the sonograms that she had when she saw him at church.

Today was Tamariane's thirty-seventh-week doctor's appointment, and, as routine, Dexter was in his room pacing back and forth, expecting her call. She generally called in the afternoon following her dates to update him. However, the afternoon had come and gone without a word from Tamariane. As he retrieved his cell phone to call her, G-ma Dye tapped on his bedroom door and entered.

"Hey, G-ma, have you heard from Tamariane or Bishop? I know she had an appointment today."

"Yes, baby, that's why I came in here."

"What did she say? How's the baby?" His eyes grew wide, seeing the worry in her eyes.

"Have a seat, my handsome boy."

"I don't want to sit down. What happened, G-ma?" His voice cracked.

"Tamariane is doing good, thank God. She went into labor this morning and was rushed to the hospital. When the medical staff checked the baby, they couldn't find a heartbeat. They did another test and confirmed the baby had died. The umbilical cord was wrapped around that poor baby's neck, son. I am so sorry."

"So, my son is dead? Is what you're saying? Why? He's innocent. He's done nothing wrong!" His cries bounced off of the walls.

"Yes, son, Bishop said God doesn't make mistakes. You two conceived the baby in sin. The sin did this, not God."

It took Dexter several weeks to mourn the loss of his son and Tamariane. Tamariane's mom moved her to Atlanta once they released her from the hospital. Bishop felt it was best for them to start anew after all that had happened. He told both of them that God had it all under control, and He'd given them a second chance to get it right. And when they have a child, whether it is with each other or someone else, everything would work together for their good. God would get the glory because they would be then right in His eyes. Bishop reiterated that God honors marriage, and that's what needed to take place *before* a child comes into the world.

Tamariane detested her grandfather's heartless response. Dexter, on the other hand, believed it had to be right because if jealousy could get Satan kicked out of heaven, then it's almost protocol for his child to be called home. Dexter agreed his son had been conceived in sin, as Bishop stated. The Man Up Above that he served wasn't the author of confusion. To Dexter, having a child at his and Tamariane's young age was loaded with turmoil and unnecessary embarrassment, and God had the last say in the matter.

Chapter Eight

The Weekend Getaway . . .

Rosalind had been attending service with the girls and the Pattersons frequently. She yearned to be around and near Naomi-Ruth. The sadness Rosalind noticed in Naomi-Ruth's eyes was recognizable. She saw it when she looked at her image in the mirror. Rosalind had never given up anything or on anyone in her life. No employer had ever fired her, and she's been working since she was 14 years old. However, five years ago, she'd been employed as the nursing supervisor at New York Presbyterian Hospital—where she was terminated for failure to renew her nursing license, which just so happened to have been two weeks after she filed charges against the director of hospital affairs, who was also the hospital's CEO's son.

Since the age of 10, Rosalind had daydreamed of being a nurse. Watching both of her parents lose their battles with cancer a year after each other, she developed a passion for helping the sick. Because Rosalind could not do anything for her parents, she had pledged to pursue a career in the health-care industry so she could do what she wasn't capable of doing as a child. All that she had worked for was taken away from her following her first overnight shift at the hospital. Rosalind covered for one of her colleagues that evening, and while taking a short break, her director, Brad, boxed her in one of the vacant rooms she used during her day shift to meditate.

The female staff members recognized Brad for his improper comments, but because he was the chief administrator's offspring, they overlooked it. No one had ever charged him of sexual mischief, so when he wandered into the room, Rosalind thought nothing of it.

"Are you in here alone?" Brad sized up the room.

"Yes, I am. I am just finishing up here. I'll be out of your way in less than a minute."

"No need." He closed in on her personal space.

"Is everything all right?" Rosalind surged to her feet.

"Everything, and I mean everything I see is fine." He licked his lips.

"I am not in the mood for your antics, Brad. It's late."

"You will be in the mood for all that I want you to be in the mood for." He wrapped his hands around her throat.

"Brad, please, stop," she pleaded a little above a whisper.

"If you scream, I'll make it worse. No one can hear you anyway. It's just you and me. Just the way you want it. That's why you came in here."

Before Rosalind could fight, Brad grabbed her by the collar and shoved her back down on the armchair she was relaxing on. He ripped her pants off and invaded her for the remaining two hours of her shift. When he was done, he used some gauze and hand soap to clear the traces of Rosalind left on him and took off. He left Rosalind to weep in despair. Confused, she dressed in a bedsheet and stumbled down the hall with no control. Everyone who looked at her realized that something drastic had happened to her. She was lost in her thoughts.

Rosalind wandered into the Emergency Room with a few of her coworkers behind her. After an examination using a rape kit and giving an account of the horrid two-hour rape, she was discharged to return home. Her manager then gave Rosalind time off, and it was then that her three-year license renewal had come—and passed. Because of her state of mind, she overlooked renewing her licensure, and the administration used it against her and ended her employment at the hospital. Rosalind elected not to seek legal action as a result because she wanted no more trouble. Her world had turned upside down. She became a victim of rape and unemployment within three weeks. She couldn't stand any further heartbreak.

It had been five years since she'd secured a job. Rosalind had been volunteering at Erwin Nursing Home. She had applied for permanent positions. However, each time a potential job has called her in for an interview, she managed not to show up.

Unbeknownst to anyone, Rosalind had been collecting public assistance to provide for herself and Desirae. The shame she encountered was harsh and severe. It had been painful for her to consider starting anew. She had been stagnant for quite a while. Her sole consolation had been volunteering at the nursing home and the girls. Following Naomi-Ruth's breakdown at the hospital, Rosalind adjusted her schedule to make sure Desirae's and her plans always included Naomi-Ruth. The ladies spent a significant amount of time at Rosalind's house instead of the Pattersons', as they did formerly. However, because Rosalind had been attending church regularly, Naomi-Ruth's parents saw no wrong in her spending time with Desirae at her home.

It had been five months since Naomi-Ruth's stay at the hospital, and she and Desirae were now on summer recess. Rosalind worked out what she did typically for the summertime and took a vacation from work, which, to her, was also known as volunteering, to devote time with Desirae and now, Naomi-Ruth. The adolescents had been begging Rosalind to take them to Hershey Park.

The weekend had finally come, and she surprised the girls with a weekend getaway to Pennsylvania. Rosalind cleared it with the Pattersons. They didn't have a problem with giving Naomi-Ruth permission to go away for a couple of days as long as Rosalind agreed to be back in time for Sunday school.

Rosalind wanted to experience the girls' first trip to Pennsylvania with them, so instead of driving, she decided they'd catch the train to Manhattan. Naomi-Ruth was overjoyed because she hadn't been on the Long Island Rail Road before, although she was born and raised on Long Island in Amityville. She had never traveled by train either. Her parents usually drove her everywhere she needed to go. She was even more ecstatic because once in the city, they would also catch a Greyhound bus from there to Pennsylvania, which was another first for Naomi-Ruth, as well as Desirae. She too had never ridden on a charter bus before.

The ladies watched movies, talked, and ate during the three-hour ride. Well, Rosalind and Desirae ate. Naomi-Ruth was getting over a stomach bug, so she didn't have much of an appetite. It disappointed her because the sight of everything made her want to devour all Rosalind had packed for them. Rosalind had loaded a cooler with drinks, sandwiches, fruit, and had the girls' favorite, fried chicken, on deck. Before they realized it, they reached their destination, unpacked, and headed to the pool in their hotel.

The water and afternoon sunlight were just what the three of them needed. All that had occurred over the previous five months made this minute worth it. Their fears, setbacks, and worries did not exist.

As Naomi-Ruth stepped out of the pool, spasms stripped the grin from her face. Cramps gripped her middle as if a thousand needles had wedged themselves into her uterus. Gasping heavily, she prayed in fear, uncertain of what was going on. Suddenly, blood gushed down her legs as contractions pulsed through her. Naomi-Ruth believed her insides had split open. A steady stream of blood poured through her, and the discomfort increased, causing her to squeal in agony.

"Nomi, what's wrong?" Desirae's heart dropped as her eyes trailed the blood. "Oh my goodness, Mom—she's bleeding!" Desirae panicked.

"Someone, please, call 911." Rosalind said, "Nomi, you will be all right. I promise."

Rosalind quickly realized what's going on with Naomi-Ruth—and it horrified her.

"Am I dying? I don't want to die." Fear rose in her eyes.

"No, baby, you are not dying."

Naomi-Ruth was rushed to Lehigh Valley Hospital. With Rosalind and Desirae at her bedside, a doctor informed her that she was four months pregnant, and because of untreated syphilis, she miscarried. As the doctor disclosed what the next few hours would involve, tears and confusion filled each of them with trepidation. Tears dropped from three sets of eyes. Rosalind's worst fears had become Naomi-Ruth's reality. She knew what had really gone on with Naomi-Ruth was tragic and wasn't at all close to what Naomi-Ruth and Desirae had insisted. What Rosalind had suspected was now weighing in on her. Her heart hammered in her chest, watching tears veil Naomi-Ruth's fearful face.

***

In Naomi-Ruth's mind, she felt she had created all that had taken place with her. Had she not disobeyed her parents and put on pants behind their backs, she would not have experienced any of this. She knew it was her fault. The further she pondered about it, the heavier she sobbed. Rosalind and Desirae tried to console her, but their words settled on deaf ears.

As soon as the medical team left the room, Desirae blubbered, "Nomi, we have to tell the truth. Look what he did to you."

"Who? Who did this to you? Please tell me. I'll fix this for you, I promise. This is not your fault, Nomi," Rosalind said.

Naomi-Ruth shook her head no in response and pulled the sheet over her face.

"He attacked her, Mommy."

"Who did, baby? Who hurt her?"

"Some guy. Some guy r-raped her after school. She didn't get jumped. Some nasty man did this to her, Mom. I'm sorry, Nomi, but I have to say something." Desirae fell apart.

Naomi-Ruth couldn't defend herself. She whimpered harder as Desirae replayed the horrific motion picture of her life that had been playing in her brain over and over for the past four months.

"I am so sorry, Nomi. He will *not* get away with this. We'll call your parents so they can press charges. Do you know who he is?"

"No! Please don't tell them. I can't tell them. Please don't. They'll blame me. I didn't even see his face. All I know is he's a big man, and he hurt me," she wailed.

"No, they won't because this is *not* your fault. You didn't have to see his face for them to know this wasn't your fault, baby. I'll be there with you every step of the way."

"It *is* my fault, and it won't matter that you're there. You heard what my mother did to me when I told her I got jumped. She'll never understand. It'll just make things worse."

"Nomi, do you understand what the doctors have to do to you? I cannot keep this from your parents. They should be here now, but I don't want to scare them. As soon as we get back, we'll sit down and talk to them."

Naomi-Ruth had to undergo a D&C, a procedure to extract the uterine lining, as a result of her miscarriage. She didn't understand all that was going on. The only thing she realized for sure is that a baby had died inside of her. The thought of it all horrified her.

After spending a day and a half of their weekend getaway hospitalized, Naomi-Ruth was released and required bed rest, penicillin, and a follow-up appointment with her primary care physician. Although Rosalind and Desirae were at her beck and call, Naomi-Ruth felt as if she were alone. She couldn't avoid the horrifying fear and powerlessness that her mind incarcerated her in. Naomi-Ruth saw no other solution to evade the tormenting feelings that bogged her down. Thoughts of death consumed her. It was by far the best alternative to facing her parents. For her, the dread of their reactions was more than she could endure.

As they pulled up to Naomi-Ruth's home, together, Naomi-Ruth's abdomen muscles started to curdle like milk left behind in the sun.

"I'd willingly die or take my own life than go in there and deal with my parents," Naomi-Ruth confessed.

"Death is never an option. I love you as if I birthed you. I will not tolerate anyone or anything that will create further injury to you. I promise you," Rosalind sniffled.

Exiting the car, the uneasiness among them intensified. By the time they made their way up the walkway, Naomi-Ruth was choking with worry. This was the most sensitive matter she'd ever had to face. It was the harshest thing any of them had to confront. Upon entering, fear immobilized Naomi-Ruth as her mom embraced her.

"How was your trip? Better yet, what's wrong? You brought a disturbing spirit in here, Ruth."

"Good afternoon, Mrs. Patterson," Rosalind interjected and breathed before proceeding. "Can we sit down and talk?"

"Sure. Is everything all right?"

Dazed with fear, Naomi-Ruth shook uncontrollably. Her feet had a mind of their own. She trembled, but her feet cemented themselves to the floor.

"What's wrong with you, Ruth?" her mom asked again, studying her.

"I think we should talk," Rosalind cut in.

As Rosalind spoke, divulging all that Naomi-Ruth had suffered, Vera roared out to God as if she were being pierced with each word that floated from Rosalind's lips. Vera sprang to her feet and rushed back to where Naomi-Ruth was standing. Already in arm's distance, she sank to her knees, hugging Naomi-Ruth's waist. Words couldn't convey the pain Vera was experiencing for her daughter. All she could do was apologize and squeeze Naomi-Ruth tighter and tighter.

"Dear God, what happened?" Levi choked up, observing his wife and daughter whimpering.

"Nomi . . . Nomi was hurt, Pastor Patterson," Desirae said, breaking down.

"Let us pray." Levi reached for his wife's hand.

"I mean no disrespect, Pastor, but why don't you love on Naomi-Ruth and pray later? She needs your love and compassion right now."

"Prayer is the answer and solution to every problem there is. Praying is a sign of my love for my family, Sister Rosalind."

"Pastor, your daughter needs more than a sign." She too broke down.

Chapter Nine

A Family that Prays . . .

Naomi-Ruth's dad, Pastor Levi Patterson, was a firm believer. He is who he is and has come as far as he has because of prayer. Had he not been able to cry to God and God not meet his prayers from the age of 12, the system or drugs would have devoured him whole. Pastor Patterson's parents were drug addicts, and often his home turned into a narcotic den. The street vendors afforded his parents their poison of choice on demand around the clock. Two or more individuals regularly took up residence in Levi's home. They became his extended family after a while. His mom and dad told him to refer to their houseguests as "aunts" and "uncles."

Levi would attend school faithfully. In fact, he looked forward to school. He hated being home watching his parents in the inebriated state they remained in. Young Levi had perfect attendance and was a straight-A pupil. He attempted to join every sport his school's athletic program provided. However, young Levi's arms and legs didn't coordinate as well as his peers'. Dribbling or pitching a ball would leave him injured without fail. His friends joined the clubs he didn't qualify for, leaving him behind to fend for himself. As a result of Levi's limited flexibility, he returned home straight after school.

Being home in the early afternoon was an experience to Levi in the beginning. Then he started to look forward to going back to see what off-the-wall situation would take place. There was always something going on. Either the purchasers were quarreling with one another, seemingly half-asleep, or one of his "aunts" or "uncles" were threatening and forcing one the customers out of the apartment. Either way, it had been more satisfying to Levi than watching television. That was . . . until one of the junkies was thrown out of the house wearing nothing but a bra and panties. Leianna had spent a significant amount of time at the house during the day. She would be there when Levi woke in the morning and when he returned from school. Levi met her on the floor, weeping outside of his apartment door.

"Are you all right?" Levi asked.

"I . . . I'm fine. Pray with me, little boy," she murmured, grabbing him by the hand.

"I don't know how to pray. We have to get you some help. Momma come—"

Leianna cut him short by putting her hand over his mouth. "Praying is the only thing that can fix things, little boy," she sniffled before going on.

"God is faithful. He always makes a plan of escape. You'll see. Close your eyes and pray. Just watch. Before we finish our prayer, your uncle Porter will open the door and let me back in."

Young Levi followed Leianna and partly closed his eyes. He was uncertain what he should be doing because he couldn't keep his 12-year-old eyes off of her. He'd never looked at a woman's unmentionables before, nor has he seen a woman as beautiful as her. She was pretty, but she appeared frail. Her skin soft, full lips, and straight nose were all perfectly connected to make her one of the most attractive women Levi had ever encountered. Her dilated pupils and the distorted glaze over her eyes alone marred her beauty.

As Leianna began to call upon her Heavenly Father and pray for forgiveness, as she said, Uncle Porter opened the door, apologized, and urged her back inside. Once inside, he draped her with a bathrobe, patted her on her backside, and directed her to tidy herself up so she wouldn't upset the churchman when he got home. Leianna was a dope fiend by day, and a preacher's wife come sunset. She had been praying about the thorn in her side, her addiction to crack, and trusted that God would deliver her in His own time.

Levi didn't understand what Uncle Porter meant when he referred to the churchman until Leianna showed up at his apartment Sunday morning with a shirt and tie for him. With his parents' permission, she took him to Sunday school and Sunday service where he met her husband, Pastor Kewin. Leianna's beauty mesmerized Levi. He stared at her the entire ride to the church house. The woman he attended church with was not the same woman who had been lying down on the floor in her unmentionables. She was in her Sunday best, and her face coated as if God Himself had applied her makeup. Levi loved the service and attended church with Leianna and her husband every time the doors opened. Leianna took to him as if he were her own. Because of her habit, each time she conceived a baby, she miscarried.

Leianna prayed a lot and taught young Levi the power of invocation. From their initial experience, he had a sense that prayer made things take place because every time Leianna asked, God produced it. After attending church for the first time with Leianna, Levi asked God if he could leave from his place of residence and live in the temple because he felt safe there. God answered his pleas, but not how he'd preferred. However, he was able to move into the church house. Leianna and her husband's apartment was alongside their church building. After the deaths of Levi's parents, Leianna moved him in with her and her husband, Pastor Kewin. She vowed to undergo substance abuse treatment so she could be the mother to Levi that he'd never really had. Levi's mother and father died of overdoses while he was in church. He didn't understand at the time why God would allow death to take his parents from him. However, as Levi matured into a man, over time, he realized their deaths were necessary for him to become the man of God that he was.

Prayer is all that Pastor Levi Patterson identified with, which is why he asked Rosalind to leave from his presence when she suggested he pray later. He also forbid Naomi-Ruth from spending time over at Rosalind's place any more. They welcomed Desirae to come over to their home whenever she wanted. However, Pastor Patterson no longer felt comfortable with his daughter hanging out over at a woman's house who had a reprobate mind. Because of her suggestion not to talk with his Heavenly Father, Levi felt Rosalind had turned her soul over to a wicked spirit. And it was the reason she hadn't attended church for so long nor cared about the things of God, such as prayer.

His primary concern was Naomi-Ruth. Learning someone had abused her innocence, and she had a miscarriage as a result crushed him. Memories of his childhood haunted him, listening to Naomi-Ruth's story. He'd watch the dealers violate some of the women that were in his apartment on one too many occasions. Pastor Patterson couldn't imagine the loves of his life suffering anything close to what he'd seen. All Levi ever wanted was to cover his wife and daughter. God hadn't allowed any harm to come near his dwelling. It was his responsibility not to let his household go through all that he'd witnessed as a child, especially his daughter. The Lord had blessed him with the honor of being her father, and it was his job to shelter her as God had protected him.

"Ruth, your momma called the mothers of the church, and we are going to meet them at the altar."

Naomi-Ruth didn't try fighting. She knew it would merely lead to matters getting worse. Besides, whenever something happened, there was *always* "a meeting at the altar." Seasoned women in the congregation were recognized as the mothers of the house of God. Experience was their advocate. They've seen it all, and their wisdom was perceived as being uncommon to the average person. Their prescription for a crisis was getting on your knees and crying out to God. This prayer took place from dusk to the rising of the sun. Naomi-Ruth was accustomed to these shut-ins, being the preacher's daughter. As much as she could recall, her father always spoke of the urgency of genuine prayer, which called for laboring before the Lord. He added that the pleas of the pure availed much, meaning, the appeals of an individual living right with God was something powerful and could heal the brokenhearted and move mountains. But you have to put your time in.

Naomi-Ruth spent thirteen hours in service. She "tarried" with the mothers, meaning she called on the name of Jesus until the Spirit of God overtook her. They prayed for her and with her, and after a while, she fell asleep on the second pew. Her dad didn't mind her sleeping while they labored before God because she was amongst the prayers while she drifted off. Naomi-Ruth awoke when the sun rose, and as she opened her eyes, her father and the mothers asked her to meet them back at the altar.

"Ruth, you know I love you with everything in me, don't you?" Pastor Patterson asked.

"Yes, Papa, I know you and Mom love me."

Vera wrapped her arms around her daughter without speaking a word and sobbed.

"Everything will be all right. God said it, and I believe it, my daughter. We have prayed everything loose, and God has healed you from the crown of your head to the soles of your feet. There is nothing, and I mean *nothing,* too hard for my God. You don't need any human-made medicine or to talk to any doctor. You are healed. Now, believe it and walk in it."

Pastor Patterson didn't believe in medication because Jesus paid it all on the cross. He said, "By His stripes you are healed, daughter." He refused to allow Naomi-Ruth to take the medication prescribed or see the therapist the doctors had recommended. The only person his daughter needed had always been there for her . . . God, who is an excellent counselor, the Everlasting Father, and Prince of Peace. She didn't need anybody or anything else.

PART TWO

In the Midst of It All . . .

Chapter Ten

It's a Personal Thing . . .

Following the passing of both of her parents, Naomi-Ruth discovered God. Not the God who her mommy and dad had introduced her to, but her own intimate relationship with The Man Above. Growing up in the Lord's house, Naomi-Ruth learned about the God Levi and Vera knew. She never got to experience Him for herself until those late nights when she was alone, and her thoughts dominated her with recollections of being abused when she was a minor. Although she was resentful toward her Heavenly Father, she talked to Him, because if she wasn't talking faith and showing that she was surviving it all, it was impossible to get a word in with her parents.

Pastor Patterson had stressed to Naomi-Ruth the urgency to believe the Word of the Lord and not worry or be shaken. Otherwise, all she would be doing was taking it out of God's hands, and He is the only one with the answer and cure. Naomi-Ruth wasn't allowed to live in the present and confess the thoughts and feelings of pain and sadness that tortured her. It was considered profane talk in her father's eyes. As a result, after being raped, she went about her everyday life . . . numb. That was, until shortly after her twenty-ninth birthday.

Naomi-Ruth used every chance she had at the Alpine Nursing Home with her mother visiting her father. Vera had just about taken up residence at her husband's bedside, which made it easy for Naomi-Ruth to come and go. She had clients to meet. They helped her maintain her sanity, keeping her mind preoccupied while dealing with the decline of her father's health.

After her rape, Naomi-Ruth devoted a tremendous amount of time combining outfits that veiled her shame and would not draw attention to her shape. She wore voluminous blouses that swept past her hips, complemented by a belt and knee-length skirts or pants. Or she'd pair either bottom with an oversized blazer. Naomi-Ruth received many compliments on her style of clothes. She fell in love with fashion. She started watching fashion shows on television and purchased magazines to study the latest trends. In order to keep her mind occupied after quitting the basketball team and no longer attending gym class, she convinced her father to allow her to help with assisting the women in the church with makeovers. Because she was attacked at school, Naomi-Ruth was allowed to have study hall in the place of gym, thanks to the principal being the husband of Vera's cousin. The Pattersons never divulged to the school the details that she'd been raped. They said she was "attacked."

Levi thought it was an excellent idea and rejoiced with pride that Naomi-Ruth had found something to keep her busy in the house of the Lord. Naomi-Ruth's dedication eventually shifted into a little business for her, and it boomed from the onset. Her keen eye for fashion enthralled many of the young adults and the mature saints. They booked her without question. It was Naomi-Ruth's natural gift. Just one glance at a potential client, and she could see what was missing from their wardrobe and what they needed. The further Naomi-Ruth explored, the more she grasped, so by the time she reached the age of 20, Levi invested in a small storefront location for her across the road from their temple. Women from local assemblies that the Pattersons fellowshipped with began to pursue Naomi-Ruth's help for themselves, their choirs, and praise teams. Her business expanded over the years, and Naomi-Ruth hired Desirae and trained her in everything she knew. The two friends became the talk of the town and ultimately had to move to a larger facility, formulating N&D's Boutique.

Desirae wanted to do something special for Naomi-Ruth as a thank-you gesture for trusting every detail of her business with her. So she planned a surprise birthday dinner. She couldn't praise Naomi-Ruth enough and sought to convey her gratitude every chance she could. Naomi-Ruth, on the other hand, thought she had to cover for Desirae and see a few of her clients because of an emergency Dez had said she had. Without question, Naomi-Ruth stopped by the nursing home first, as Desirae knew she would, to see her father before making her way to their boutique. When she arrived at his room, neither Levi nor Vera was in their usual spot.

Naomi-Ruth's eyes widened as her heart hammered in her rib cage. A wave of adrenaline surged through her entire being, causing steady thumps to smack the marble tile beneath her feet as she made her way to the nurses' station.

"H-hello . . . hello, my dad, where . . . Where is he?"

"Good evening, Naomi-Ruth. I'm your dad's nurse for the evening. My name is Damietta. I can see the worry in your face. Please know he's okay. Your parents chose to have dinner alone in the recreational hall."

"Is he in his bed? He's too weak to walk or stand. Can you show me where they are? He should be resting and taking it easy, not in a dining room, or whatever you called it."

"He insisted on sitting in a wheelchair, and it is actually a good thing for him to sit up and not be constrained to the bed, especially since he feels up to it."

"How could he insist on anything when he can't even speak? He has that thing in his throat." Her lips trembled.

"Even with the trachea tube, Mr. Patterson can be very persistent."

Naomi-Ruth ignored Damietta to not take her annoyance out on her. She couldn't figure out why anyone thought it would be a good idea to move Levi from his room. He was battling prostate cancer for the past year and a half and was bed bound with a trachea tube. Although Pastor was alert, his body turned against him. Naomi-Ruth sobbed daily because she felt her father became a prisoner inside his own body.

While ministering during Sunday service, Pastor Patterson had collapsed and stopped breathing. They instantly rushed him to the Emergency Room. Once the medical team obtained a pulse, they placed him on a ventilator to assist with his breathing, which was also when Vera and Naomi-Ruth learned of Levi's condition. They diagnosed him with stage four prostate cancer and with fluid around an enlarged heart. After fourteen days of being on the vent, a tracheotomy had been performed, and Levi had it in ever since.

Already down the hallway, Naomi-Ruth overheard chatter the closer they got to the recreation room. Looking in Damietta's direction, her face twisted into a grimace. Damietta smiled and opened the double doors leading into the area.

"Surprise!" everyone shouted as she entered.

"Oh my goodness," Naomi-Ruth sobbed.

Looking at her parents, Desirae, Rosalind, her close friends, a few clients, and staff in attendance made Naomi-Ruth whimper like a teething baby. She was so filled with emotions that she couldn't talk. Her eyes bounced around the room, admiring the delicacies comprising all one could think of or desire, like chicken, fish, and curried chickpeas. Whatever the adopted lifestyle, there was a dish or two to accommodate it. The décor screamed Naomi-Ruth. She had an obscene obsession with rose gold, and Desirae made sure everything included a sprinkle of it.

"Before we start, your dad has something he'd like to say." Desirae took her by the hand and led her closer to Levi.

Naomi-Ruth stared at her, puzzled and confused because everybody was aware of Levi's condition.

Although he looked uncomfortable, frail, and deteriorated, Levi smiled, staring at his beloved child. Because the rehabilitation and nursing facility knew it was only a matter of time before he would transition home to heaven, they permitted the small gathering. The owner of the facility, Edward Walbridge, was a long-standing member of the Pattersons' church, so he'd insisted on making sure everything went according to plan.

"We love you so much," Vera fumbled over her words.

"I love you more, Mom and Dad," Naomi-Ruth returned with a kiss to each of their faces.

"Your dad prepared something that he wants me to read, Ruth." She took her by the hand before continuing. "This is going to be hard for me, so please bear with my blubbering as I read," Vera confessed before proceeding.

"*This birthday is unusual for me and you, my precious Naomi-Ruth because it will be the last time we can honor your life together. I love you and your mom with all in me. Please forgive me for not protecting you as I should have. I did the best I could with what I had, and that was God. He kept me. I know He has and will continue to keep you. My methods may look off, but we are where we are now because of His grace and mercy. I call for you to remember love has no loopholes. That consists of loving yourself. God's love is unrestricted, so you have to cherish yourself the same way. You cannot unlock your future if you're handcuffed to your history. It's not about what you suffered, what was taken from you, or what you have left behind anymore. Right now, the only thing that counts is how you make it all work for you.*

"You realize we couldn't determine what name we wished for you because we admired the meaning of both, which is how we came up with Naomi-Ruth. The beginning of your name, Naomi, means pleasantness, and Ruth is something worth seeing and a friend of God. You are exceptional, Naomi-Ruth. God will take all the pain you've been through and turn it into wind beneath your wings to haul you into your next level. From this day forward, I want you to live and not die. I love you and want you to make me proud by becoming the pleasant wife, mother, daughter, and friend of God that I destined you to be.

"Love always, your Poppa Levi."

Three days following Naomi-Ruth's birthday, Levi took his last breath with Vera and her by his side. It was another slap to Naomi-Ruth's emotional state. She'd prayed and believed God's Word for Levi. Her father was supposed to have pulled through. They served a healing God. Fasting, praying, and shunning wine, her guilty pleasure, as she referred to it, hadn't worked. Naomi-Ruth felt forsaken by God. There wasn't anything anyone could convey to her to make her see things differently.

Pacing back and forth in her bedroom, Naomi-Ruth begrudgingly challenged her Heavenly Father. "God, I don't understand how people can shift their lives over to you when you allow us to suffer no matter what. We give up everything and still lose the ones that we love. How is this possible? You stated you wouldn't allow any harm to come near our dwelling. I got on my knees and talked to you more than I ever have the whole time my dad was ill. I fasted for days, and yet, you took him. You're supposed to know me better than I know myself. My dad said part of my name means a friend of God. You know my name, God, and if I am your friend, how could you do this to me? The Bible says unreliable friends would come to ruin, but you are a friend that sticks closer than a brother, and yet, you abandoned me like an untrustworthy friend."

"*Ruth!*" Vera interrupted her.

"M-mom . . . Mom, I didn't hear you come in. How long have you been standing there? Please sit down. You look so fragile and fatigued," she sniffled.

"I overheard you in my bedroom. You're furious with God, Ruth, when you shouldn't be."

"Why? Oh, because Papa isn't suffering any longer? Well, if God would have healed him, he would not have gone through any of what he went through."

"That's not accurate at all. Your dad has been sick for a long time—"

"Mom, I know. I was there."

"Please allow me to finish. Doctors diagnosed your father years before the disease spread throughout his body. He and I believed the Word, and Jesus' stripes healed him. It is possibly a little too late for me now as well, but I learned we are healed, as the Word says. However, faith without works is dead. God had equipped us with the tools we needed to use to bring the healing to pass. Doctors, medicine, and even healthier lifestyles were accessible to us for a reason. We had to use wisdom and take advantage of what God had set before us. Many of us leave this world ignorant because we only take parts of the Word and apply it to our lives. I am a victim of that same ignorance and haven't been in the strongest of health either. Instead of pursuing medical attention,

I too thought I was already restored instead of working so my healing could work for me. That's why your daddy is no longer with us, Ruth. God did His part, baby. Your papa and I didn't do ours. So, if I leave here tomorrow, I want you to know that *none* of this is the Lord's fault. We rushed the process."

Two weeks after the demise of Pastor Patterson, his dear widow, Vera, joined him in paradise. She'd gone to sleep and didn't wake up again. Vera usually woke before Naomi-Ruth and prepared breakfast as she had all of her life. When Naomi-Ruth didn't see her sitting at the kitchen table, she went to Vera's room, thinking she'd overslept. Vera's tired heart took a long night's sleep into eternal rest. She suffered from hypertension and had a heart attack while asleep. Naomi-Ruth noticed her mother was gone the moment she opened the bedroom door. Her body quivered as she made her way to Vera's bedside.

Taking her mom by the hand, Naomi-Ruth prayed through tears and spoke to Vera simultaneously. "God, I recognize my momma is in a better place. She's right where she desired to be with you and my papa. Momma, I am going to be all right. Sleep easy and tell Papa I love him. You two take care of each other until I see you again. Neither of you has to suffer anymore. I will make you proud and keep the new pastor in line. I'm in a better place psychologically, so you don't have to worry about me, Momma. You prepared me for that. I know all I need to know to make it without you here. I don't know what tomorrow holds, Momma, but what I *do* know is that I will be all right. I'm sure you and Poppa will look down on me, making sure I am good. Dear God, I ask that you bless my momma's soul and receive her into your loving arms. In Jesus' name, I pray. Amen."

That evening, Naomi-Ruth had her initial intimate experience with God. As if she had an out-of-body experience, the Lord appeared to her in a dream. While in her slumber, she looked at herself, lying in her bed, mourning for her parents, identical to what she was doing when she wandered off to sleep. Naomi-Ruth recited the same prayer she'd prayed before sleep absorbed her whole.

"Heavenly Father, I realized I need you more today than I did yesterday. I want more of you and less of me. There's no way I will get through any of this without you. My momma is no longer here. It's just you and me. Show me your glory. I can't live right or another day without it."

"I've been here all the time. I said I would never leave you or forsake you. I will keep you in perfect peace. Keep your mind stayed on me. I am the Lord thy God, and beside me, there is no other," a still voice whispered in her ear.

Naomi-Ruth jumped from her sleep and examined her room, looking for the voice she'd heard in her ear. Tears masked her countenance as she recognized it was a dream. Naomi-Ruth thanked God for listening to her and coming to her in her time of need. It all seemed surreal, but she could feel a strength that she hadn't felt before. She had a peace of mind and knew that, without a doubt, everything would be all right, no matter what.

Chapter Eleven

He Proposed to Me . . .

Desirae and Rosalind were pretty much all of the family Naomi-Ruth had left outside of her church family. However, before Naomi-Ruth took on Desirae as a partner at Ruth's Boutique, there was a strain on their friendship. When Pastor Patterson forbade Naomi-Ruth from spending time over at Rosalind's place, she, in turn, ceased all communication with the Pattersons, including Naomi-Ruth. It'd broken her heart, but she didn't feel comfortable with Desirae spending time over at someone's house who held ill feelings toward her. Desirae fought against her mother's wishes initially and went behind her back and did the opposite of Rosalind's demands.

When Desirae knew Rosalind was long gone and on her way to work, she'd spend the afternoon after school at the Pattersons while her mom was at work. Rosalind had found part-time employment at the nursing home she volunteered at and continued volunteering in the off-hours. She enjoyed caring for the elderly and took pleasure in all she undertook for them. After taking ill one afternoon, Rosalind retired early from her shift. Feeling dizzy after vomiting violently, she mustered up as much strength that she could to make it home so she could get herself situated and make sure Desirae was all right. However, when she pulled up into her driveway, she saw Desirae sitting on the Pattersons' front porch chatting with Naomi-Ruth.

"Dez, what did I tell you?" Rosalind scolded her, exiting her car.

"Mm, I—"

"I don't want to hear anything! You know what I told you! Get in this house!"

Storming through the door, Desirae exploded, "Why do I have to suffer because you and Pastor don't get along? We are the kids, and y'all act like us, not speaking to one another. This is so stupid. I—"

Before Desirae could finish her sentence, Rosalind's hand connected with the right side of her face. "Now, go to your room! I don't know who you think you're talking to, but you're about to—"

The balance of her lunch cut her sentence short as it spewed out, soiling the tips of her shoes and the hardwood floor beneath her.

"That's what she gets for hitting me," Desirae mumbled, slamming her bedroom door shut.

She knew because Rosalind wasn't feeling well, she would get away with slamming the door. Had it been any other time, she would have felt whatever the hinges of the door frame might feel when a door is shut hard.

"Consider yourself on punishment," Rosalind threatened from the other side of the door in passing.

Because Naomi-Ruth had begged Desirae to come over and ignore Rosalind's orders, she was livid with Naomi-Ruth. When they entered school the next morning, Desirae lit into Naomi-Ruth.

"It's *your* fault I'm on punishment. Your parents think they are better than my mom, and that's why you can't come over," Desirae barked.

"You know that's not true, Dez. Now, take it back."

"I thought about it last night, and it *is* true. That's the only reason your father said you couldn't come over. I don't know why I listened to you. You're a fake friend, church girl."

"Don't call me that, Dez. You know I hate when people call me that."

"I'm not taking anything back. It's the truth, little church girl."

"That's it." Naomi-Ruth dropped her books, charged Desirae, and shoved her into the lockers along the wall.

Within moments, the two friends who'd been inseparable and tied at the hip were rolling on the floor, kicking, punching, and pulling each other's hair. They were acting like they didn't know each other.

The Pattersons and Rosalind struggled to swallow their anger after hearing the girls had had a fistfight and had been suspended from school. Rosalind couldn't accept Naomi-Ruth's actions and took it out on Levi and Vera when they showed up at the school following the altercation.

"Excuse me. Can I speak to you before we go inside?"

"Sure," Levi responded.

"What kind of preacher are you? Your daughter struck my child because of name-calling. But I am not surprised because when situations don't go your way, you assault as well. This is an example that the fruit didn't fall far from that tree." She rolled her eyes.

Desirae had called Rosalind in hysterics to lessen her punishment by telling her Naomi-Ruth had tackled her into the lockers.

"I have never assaulted you, Rosalind. No weapon formed against me or my household shall prosper, and any tongue that rises against us in judgment shall be condemned. Now, if you have nothing uplifting to say, please excuse us." He marched toward the school building with Vera on his heels.

Each time Levi used the Word to speak to Rosalind, it troubled her as if he'd struck her because she felt like he was chastising her. As a result of this confrontation, Rosalind said she'd had enough of the Pattersons and found a condo in another part of the city in a different school district. Naomi-Ruth and Desirae never reconciled things because they didn't see each other after the transfer. It was as if they lived in separate states because they didn't run into each other at all.

Desirae resented Rosalind's decision to move after a while. She didn't want to meet new people and start over as "the new kid." Without question, she missed Naomi-Ruth, but she refused to make the first move and call her. Naomi-Ruth didn't put forth any effort either. Their stubbornness forced them to grow apart over time.

Dez started hanging around two sisters whose parents were never home, and when they were there, it was as if they weren't. They supported their twin daughters, Monica and Monique, in living carefree lives at 16. As long as it was in the garage, they were able to smoke marijuana and drink alcohol. Their parents even permitted them to have boys over but only in the garage.

Desirae spent time hanging out at Monica and Monique's place while their parents were home. Rosalind trusted Desirae under their supervision without getting to know them outside of the initial introduction she'd received while grocery shopping. Omar and Latrine both worked nine-to-five jobs—the father as a maintenance director and the mother as a housekeeper by day—and their nights consisted of hosting intimate cocaine parties in their master suite.

Latrine made sure she prepared breakfast before the girls left for school, and dinner was on the table every night. They even sat down together as a family for dinner just about every day. However, family time concluded by seven o'clock sharp in the evening on party nights. The twins weren't aware of what their parents were involved in. They just knew they had to have their homework completed before Omar and Latrine had their "alone time." From the outside looking in, they were upstanding parents, which they were, but they also enjoyed their "snow parties."

The only things Desirae was familiar with were the church and Rosalind spoiling her by taking her shopping, out to dine, or on a weekend getaway. She knew nothing about smoking or drinking. She was a virgin to all of it, including intercourse. Monica and Monique could be looked at as experts in all areas as they'd been dibbling and dabbling in everything since they were 14. Things transformed and took a turn for the worse during Desirae's second week at the twins' "G-room," the name Monica and Monique had named the garage. Their dad had changed the car storage area into a hangout suite for his daughters. He'd had a restroom installed, and to accommodate his little ladies, he installed a 55-inch television, sofa, love seat, and a pool table for their enjoyment.

Desirae's first experience with getting drunk and high made her uneasy the first couple of minutes. She knew Rosalind would be disappointed if she ever found out, but Desirae's mind was too far gone into her new life. Once the nervousness subsided, she started liking the pleasure that took over her. Everything was amusing, and nothing mattered any longer. Even while in the company of the three young guys, Desirae danced to the beat of her drum. She sashayed around the suite with and without music. It was her first time meeting the boys. Two of them were the twins' boyfriends, and the third guy was their friend, Garrett.

Without an invitation, Garrett followed Desirae to the restroom. As she attempted to close the door behind her, he used his foot to prevent it from shutting.

"Umm, excuse your foot. I got here first. You have to wait."

"I just want to watch."

"That is *nasty!* Who wants to see someone use the bathroom?"

"I don't want to see someone. I want to see *you*. I like you."

"You don't even know me."

"I know what I like, and I like what I see, and what I see is you."

Desirae felt weird and sought to cover her blush behind her fingers.

"Don't you dare hide that pretty smile from me." Garrett pulled her hands from her face.

Before she could protest, he managed to make his way into the bathroom. He locked eyes with her without letting her hand loose and eased in. As if she were in a trance, Desirae backed up and followed his lead, allowing him entrance. Shame filled her as the door shut. She was unable to keep eye contact. Desirae's gaze skittered around the room, looking at everything *but* him.

"There you go again, getting bashful on me. But little do you know, it's only going to make me like you even more. You're nothing like your friends. You're special, Desirae. You are special just for me. Can I have you as mine, beautiful?"

"You cannot have any part of me until I'm married. I have to be married before I give my mind or body to someone, and I'm too young. Besides, I don't even know you."

At five foot three and thick, Desirae had the body of a much-older girl. Her smooth, brown skin stretched over her large C-cup breasts, wide hips, and a juicy behind. Desirae's pretty face complimented the package that mesmerized Garrett. Normally, she disliked the attention she received because of her figure. However, Garrett's close-cut wavy hair, cinnamon skin, and light, dreamy eyes had her feeling tingly on the inside. She had never felt or reacted to a male's presence or attention until Garrett's tall, somewhat-lanky frame and baritone voice mesmerized her.

Four years her senior, Garrett was hesitant when the twins suggested he meet their friend. However, the moment he saw Desirae, everything he believed in went out the window. He had to have her. He frowned on dating younger girls, but he knew Desirae was different.

"Well, it looks like we're getting married. I'm not allowing you to get away from me."

Garrett meant what he said in that bathroom. He waited for Desirae for two years. On her eighteenth birthday, he met her at the G-room and asked her to marry him. They spent time together almost every day before that getting to know each other outside of sex. Desirae kept Rosalind in the dark the entire time. Although she had suspicions that Desirae either had a crush or was possibly trying to get to know someone, Rosalind had no clue what was going on with her daughter and Garrett until the proposal.

"Mom!" Desirae shouted, charging through the door, holding Garrett's hand.

"What is all the screaming about, girl?" Rosalind came out of the kitchen.

"This is Garrett, Mom. We're getting married."

"You're getting *what?* I'm going to need your lanky ass to get the hell out of my house." She pointed to Garrett before directing her attention back to Desirae. "Dez, have you lost your damn mind?"

"My apologies, Miss Rosalind."

"Please go." Rosalind opened the door.

As the door shut behind Garrett, Desirae screamed, "This is what I want, Mom! I am old enough to get married without your permission."

"You're not old enough to wash your tail correctly. Don't let that boy play with your mind, and you end up making the same mistake I made."

"Just because you're lonely and pathetic doesn't mean I'll be the same way."

Fury drove Rosalind to the unthinkable. Jerking her hand back, slapped Desirae's face, causing her head to slam into the wall behind her.

"I hate you!" Desirae shouted, running to her room and slamming the door behind her.

Rosalind wasn't happy with hitting Desirae. However, she didn't regret what she did, either. In her eyes, Dez was disrespectful, and she refused to permit any form of disrespect. Instead of going behind her offspring, Rosalind gave herself and Dez space to cool off. She understood Desirae was 18, but her baby girl was still learning herself. Marriage was the last thing that should be on her mind. If Rosalind could choke Garrett, she would do just that. She shook her head in displeasure seeing that Garrett was noticeably older than Dez. After she sat down and spoke to her daughter, Rosalind planned to set Garrett in his place and press charges if she had too.

Unfortunately, Rosalind allowed too much time to pass. She'd awaken early to prepare breakfast and have Dez come down to eat and talk, but when Rosalind went to her room to wake her . . . Desirae wasn't there. She left during the night to be with her fiancé, Garrett.

Chapter Twelve

Why Did I Get Married . . . ?

To Rosalind, Desirae was a well mannered child who gave her no problems. She wasn't aware of Dez's extra-curricular activities that she'd indulged in at the G-room. Turning 18 gave Desirae a newfound mind-set, and love was all she cared about. But it just wasn't any love. She wanted Garrett's love. For the two years, she and Garrett dated, Desirae concluded she could do whatever she wanted when she turned legal. Garrett stressed the fact that he would marry her once Desirae came of age. She made sure to abide by Rosalind's rules even when she didn't agree with them because the only thing that mattered to Dez was being with Garrett.

At 22, from the outside looking in, Garrett had it going on for himself. He was a college student with his own car and apartment and a part-time job as a cabin service cleaner for an airline, where he worked at night. However, already under the same roof and now attending the same college as her husband, Desirae found out proof of the pudding was in the eating. Garrett's apartment was in the basement of his mother's home, and his car and insurance were in her name. The only things Desirae didn't find conflict with was the fact that Garrett attended class and faithfully went to work. Since they'd married, he had picked up more hours at work. At least, that's what he had told her why he'd been away from home so much.

After whisking away Desirae in the night, they went to the courthouse and eloped. He was delighted to bring his bride home after longing for her for two years. Garrett attempted to take Desirae the moment he carried her across the threshold. Although Dez now saw a grown woman looking back at her, the coy and reserved girl Rosalind gave birth to manifested. As Garrett sought to become one with his wife, Desirae's insecurities frustrated him.

"Dezzy, baby, I promise to be gentle, so please try to relax. I know this is your first time, but I waited so long for this."

"Is this the only thing you waited for?" She tightened her grip on the towel, covering her nudity.

"We just got married, so why would I have married you just for sex? That doesn't make sense, does it?"

While dating, Garrett had never made it past second base. Kissing, groping, and petting were all that had taken place. And that had only happened when they were fully clothed. Desirae pushed Garrett's hands off of her when he attempted any actual skin-to-skin contact in her private areas.

"I know I'm just nervous."

Garrett pulled her closer to him, and Desirae's nerves caused her hand to tremble, and her towel dropped. Before he could admire his wife, she ran into the bathroom and locked the door behind her.

"Dezzy, what are you doing in there? Open the door! This marriage won't work if you act like you're still 16. You're a woman now, and it's time for you to act like one."

"I need more time. Please give me tonight to get myself together. Everything is happening too fast," she sniffled from the other side of the door.

"This is crazy as hell. We've been at this for hours. The damn day is gone. I need air. I'll be back later." Garrett grabbed his clothes from the floor.

Hearing the door close behind him, Desirae came out of the bathroom. Her nerves got the best of her, causing her mind to race. Parts of her wanted to go back home to her room, where she felt safe, and the other side of her mind had convinced her she wasn't little Dez any longer. With that, she straightened up Garrett's one-bedroom apartment and searched the refrigerator, hoping to make it up to him by having breakfast prepared in the morning. She wanted to be asleep by the time he returned and to rise before he woke.

As Desirae wished, Garrett was on the sofa asleep when she rose from her slumber. She attempted to carry out her plan and make it up to her husband and prepare breakfast. Unfortunately, Rosalind had made cooking look easy and may have sheltered Desirae a bit too much because the smell of smoke woke Garrett instead of the eggs she attempted to prepare.

"What in the world are you trying to do? You want us to get kicked out? My mom doesn't even know you're down here, for God's sake."

"I wanted to surprise you. I'm sorry." Her lips trembled.

"Just get out of the kitchen." He shook his head.

"Wait! Your mom doesn't know I'm here? Is *that* what you said?"

"Relax. I didn't get a chance to tell her yet. She's a little weird with stuff sometimes, so I have to ease this on her."

"Garrett, we are *married*. How the hell are you going to *ease* me on her? Why didn't she know before I moved in or before we got married?"

"The same reason you kept me a secret from your mother," he snapped.

"I'm sure she hears us down here by now, especially since you're not using your inside voice. So, why don't we go talk to her now?"

"No, we will do it on *my* terms, *not* yours. *I* am the man of this house, and we will do what *I* say. Besides, she's used to women being down here, so that won't alarm her. The fact that we're married and you've moved in is the hard part."

"Wait. She's *used* to women being down here? What is *that* supposed to mean, Garrett?"

"It means the only virgin standing in this apartment is *you.*"

That was the first of many disagreements that the newlyweds had. If it wasn't Desirae's insecurities when it came to sex, it was her not being able to cook, or the women that came by unannounced. After a while, Garrett gave up on trying to have sex with Desirae because he felt there was always one excuse after another. He regretted his decision to wait for or marry her, and they grew apart over time. Garrett spent a great deal of time away from home and covered it up with work. He no longer desired Desirae and sought comfort in other women. They were women he'd spent time with while he and Desirae dated. The straw that broke the camel's back for both of them was the day his mom, Alina, met her son's wife.

In an attempt to have a romantic dinner and feeling comfortable with allowing Garrett to bed her after being married for six months, Desirae took a stab at preparing a steak dinner. Garrett was due home in a few hours, so Desirae scurried around getting herself and the rest of the dinner prepared. She'd already placed the frozen steaks in the oven in the morning shortly after Garrett had left for class. She knew they had to thaw out and turned the oven on and placed the meat inside after seasoning it with salt.

While taking a shower, the sound of the smoke detector startled her, causing her to lose her balance in the shower. She was able to catch herself from falling and ran out to try to get things under control. Smoke smacked her in the face as the bathroom door opened. It blurred her vision so that she could not see much before her.

"I know this boy didn't leave this damn stove on!" a female screamed.

"Who's that?" Desirae asked.

"This is *my* home. *I'm* the only one who should be asking questions. Where is my son, and did he leave you here to burn my house down?"

"No, ma'am. I apologize. I was trying to surprise him with dinner. I'm sorry we had to finally meet like this, although I am glad to meet you finally."

"Who are you?"

"I am Desirae. Garrett said you were ill, and he didn't want to bombard you with meeting anyone new, but I'm his wife."

"His *what?* Girl, have you and my son have lost your minds? *Wife?* He can't even take care of himself or his responsibilities."

"I've been looking for part-time work so I can help out. I apologize if we've been a burden, ma'am."

"So, you're going to help with his child support payments and help get diapers for the boys?"

"Child support? Diapers?"

"Child, where is your mother? My son has some growing up to do, and so do you. Let me tell you something. Don't ever get yourself tied up to no man, woman, or anything until you've taken the time to get to know them. But, first, you have to know yourself. You knew something wasn't right. How long have you been here?"

"We've been married six months, ma'am."

"And you were all right with being down here, knowing I was upstairs, and you *never* saw or spoke to me?"

"I was trying to be submissive like Garrett asked me to be by respecting his wishes and doing things when he was ready."

"Baby, submissive and stupid are two different things. Is your mother still around?"

"Yes, she is, ma'am."

"Call her and go home. You're a beautiful girl and have some growing up to do. Don't allow my son's shit to have you walking around here stinking. I love my child, but he's *my* problem, so *don't* make him yours. I can't afford to take care of another person either. Go home to your mother, baby."

Rosalind had been sick to her stomach since Desirae left. She had no idea where she could be. She was with Garrett, of course, but where? Her initial thought was to go by Monica and Monique's place, and when she did, neither of them had any idea where Desirae was. The last time they'd spoken to Dez was when Garrett proposed. Desirae had cut everyone off because she didn't want anyone telling her what to do. She'd left her cell phone in her bedroom the night she disappeared with Garrett. The only thing Rosalind thought to do was what Pastor Patterson had taught her to do, which was to pray. She disliked his methods of discipline, but she admired them the same. Rosalind's thoughts tormented her at a terrifying rate. With no one to turn to, it took her just about the six months during Dez's absence to swallow her pride and call over to the Pattersons.

After apologizing, Rosalind disclosed everything that had transpired with Desirae to Levi and Vera. Without a second thought, Pastor Patterson suggested they pray. He rebuked every assignment of attack that might be on Desirae's life and told Rosalind to take God at His Word because her daughter would be back home. Pastor Patterson was on point with his words because two days after they'd spoken, Desirae called, crying.

"Mom, I messed up. I'm sorry. I can't do this anymore. Garrett is a liar. Can I come home, please?"

"Of course, you can, baby girl. Where are you? I'll come and get you right now."

Alina had brought Desirae upstairs to call and wait for Rosalind to pick her up. While upstairs, Desirae had the chance to see Garrett's twin boys, Ethan and Allen. They were miniature versions of Garrett. Their mom wanted nothing to do with them or Garrett and had dropped them at Alina's doorstep when they were 8 days old. Alina had been caring for them ever since. Because they had her DNA, she refused to allow anything to happen to her grandchildren. A mother knows her child, and Alina knew Garrett was extremely immature to care for the boys, so she took on the responsibility. Alina took her son to court so that his child support was taken out of his paycheck. If he quit his job or fell behind on his obligation, she warned Garrett she'd take him back to court until they revoked his license and arrested him if it came down to it. Alina knew the only way to get through to her son was through the courts, so she'd done just that, hoping to teach him how to take care of someone other than himself. His dad wasn't in the picture after conception, so Alina had done the best she could with what she had in raising her son.

Desirae left before Garrett came back home, and the only time they spoke after that was for the annulment of their marriage. When she returned home, Rosalind had a surprise waiting for her. Rosalind would never understand how or why Desirae jumped and got married. She did understand Monica and Monique had a strong influence on the transformation of Dez. When Rosalind went searching for Dez, Omar and Latrine directed her to the G-room to see if Desirae was down there. Then everything made sense to her. Rosalind's stomach surged in her spine when she saw the alcohol and the stench of marijuana that infiltrated her nostrils as soon as they opened the door for her.

Rosalind was a firm believer you are the company you keep. To help her daughter out and to reach a place she knew she could not reach, Rosalind asked Naomi-Ruth to come by and be at the house when Desirae got there. Desirae, on the other hand, sobbed the entire way home. She tried apologizing, but her words lodged in her throat on each attempt. Rosalind pitied her daughter and cried alongside her.

As Rosalind and Dez made their way to the door, Desirae screeched as if she'd been struck.

"Nomi, is that really you?" Desirae collapsed in Naomi-Ruth's arms.

"Yes, it's me. I've missed you so much," she cried.

The girls stayed up most of the night, catching up between crying and apologizing. They picked up where they'd left off without skipping a beat. Naomi-Ruth invited Desirae to help her with her boutique between classes. Desirae was honored and happy at the same time. It was what she needed to get her mind off of Garrett. Since finding out about his children and the other women, Desirae was beating herself up for running off into the night without a plan but primarily for rushing into this situation and not getting to know Garrett. She felt she only knew him in an impaired state. When they married, she hadn't touched alcohol or smoked weed. While in a sober state, the last thing she wanted was for Garrett to touch her. She didn't even find him as attractive as she had upon meeting him, which is why it was so difficult for her to give herself to him.

Desirae was thankful for her mother allowing her to come home and her being there.

Chapter Thirteen

My Dad's Clone . . .

Naomi-Ruth felt she was forever indebted to Desirae and Rosalind. Because of them, she was able to get through the passing of her parents. Desirae took on things at N&D's Boutique, making sure everything ran smoothly in Naomi-Ruth's absence. Rosalind kept her apprised of everything that was going on at the church. Since Desirae had returned home, Rosalind found her way back to the house of God and dedicated the majority of her time there.

When Pastor Patterson was too ill, he invited several preachers to host revivals at the church. One of the guest speakers reminded him of himself when he was younger, so he asked him to fill in as the interim pastor until he was well enough to shepherd his flock again. Shortly thereafter, Pastor Patterson's health took a turn for the worse, leaving the church without a head pastor. Levi left everything to Naomi-Ruth in the event something that something were to happen to him and Vera. She knew she wasn't in any position to pastor, so she adhered to her father's wishes with his replacement.

Dexter Lewis had come highly recommended by Levi's good friend, Bishop Livingston. Pastor Patterson was leery in the beginning learning Dexter's age, but because Bishop had vouched for Pastor Lewis, he overlooked his age. The saints took to Pastor Lewis as if he were Levi. He too preached the unadulterated Word of God. Like Pastor Patterson, Dexter stood firm on the Word of God. He preached holiness or hell.

Some of the single women in the congregation went out of their way to throw themselves at Pastor Lewis. They'd bring breakfast, lunch, and on most occasions, dinner to him. Sunday mornings, they scheduled counseling sessions and went out of their way to have a conversation with him after each service. He'd ignore their advances. Naomi-Ruth is who he had his eye on from the first time they met. When she left her father's office at the time of their meeting, Dexter asked Pastor Patterson for his blessing to marry Naomi-Ruth in the near future.

"Pastor, can I ask you a question?" Dexter inquired.

"Sure, son, what is it?"

"The Bible states that he who finds a wife finds a good thing. I believe I've found my good thing."

"Is that so, son?"

"Tell me about her."

"Tell you about my Naomi-Ruth, is that right?" Levi caught on.

"Yes, Pastor Patterson. Your Naomi-Ruth is my wife. I apologize if I am out of line, but God showed me her in a dream. I just never met her in person until today. So, what I am asking is for your blessing to marry her one day."

"Son, when that day comes, ask me again, and I'll give you an answer. Right now, you're on an assignment to preach, not mate."

Naomi-Ruth was oblivious to the conversation Dexter had with her father as well as his feelings toward her. She thought he was a very attractive young man and a well-versed preacher like her dad. However, her respect for him wouldn't allow her mind to wander too far. Naomi-Ruth had the same admiration for Pastor Lewis as she did her father. Although Levi was her dad, when it was time for church, he was Pastor Patterson, which is how she trained her mind to view Dexter. He was her pastor.

Desirae and Naomi-Ruth were the Singles' Ministry leaders. They organized outings, workshops, and conferences for the singles to gather. Without thinking about it, Naomi-Ruth invited Pastor Lewis to join one of the ministry's outings.

"Hey, Pastor Lewis, are you busy?" She peeked her head into his office.

"I'm not busy at all, Naomi-Ruth. Come on in."

"I don't mean to bother you, but we are having a volley ball tournament tonight. It'll be the men against the women. If you're not too busy, you should join us."

"I saw the flyer. This is for the Singles' Ministry, correct?"

"Yes, it is. If I'm out of line, I apologize. It's just I didn't ever see a ring on your finger or a spouse around. Other than Mother Diane, there haven't been any other women around you. I know she still wears a wedding band and has no husband. I'm going on and on. Please forgive me. I have no place inviting you."

"No apology necessary. I think I'm the one that owes you an apology. I'm sorry that I gave off signs that I am not married. I'm not sure when or how, but I lost my ring some time ago, and my wife has been out of the country on business."

"Oh my goodness. I had no idea. Everyone said you were single. Again, Pastor, please forgive me. I will never jump to conclusions and judge a book by its cover again or listen to someone else. Wow, I am so sorry."

Unable to conceal his laughter any longer, Dexter burst out laughing. Holding his chest, he confessed, "If you could see the look on your face, you'd be laughing too. I was joking, Naomi-Ruth. I am not married yet. I am as single as you'd like me to be," he flirted.

Naomi-Ruth's face burned with embarrassment as she turned to leave. Before closing the door behind her, she popped her head back in and said, "I guess I will see you then."

She had heard what Pastor Lewis said. It was just hard for her to digest. Pastor Lewis had blatantly flirted with her, and this time, she hadn't imagined things. On occasion, Naomi-Ruth thought she'd spotted him staring at her, then breaking eye contact and looking away when she caught him. However, she dismissed it, thinking she'd imagined things. At this moment, there was no denying it. Pastor Dexter Lewis was toying with her. And every occasion they were around each other alone and periodically in group settings, he'd use that same charismatic charm to cause butterflies to swirl in her stomach. The first text from him blew Naomi-Ruth's mind.

Hey, Sister Naomi, I was wondering if you knew what the weather would be.

Why would he ask me about the weather when he has a television and a phone? Oh my goodness, he's flirting with me, she assumed to herself.

Naomi-Ruth didn't reply and waited until she saw Pastor Lewis at the auxiliary meeting in the afternoon. Even though it was evident what was going on, she nevertheless had a hard time wrapping her mind around it all. Asking what the weather would be had her shaking her head every time she thought about it. She always arrived early to prepare the agenda for the meetings, and when she got there this time, Pastor Lewis was sitting in her office.

"Hh . . . Hey, Pastor. Can I help you with something? Is everything all right?"

"Well, I have a leather jacket on, and it is 80 degrees out. I have been waiting for you to get back to me on the weather forecast for today."

"Pastor, it is 2:00 in the afternoon. You mean to tell me you never thought about turning on the television or looking in your phone for it?"

"What if I told you I didn't have a television, and my phone only works on Wi-Fi, and I don't have that either."

"There I go putting my foot in my mouth again. I apologize, Pastor. Do you want me to look now for you? Wait a minute. You just said it was 80 out, so you know."

"I got you again." He roared with laughter.

"You know, maybe you missed your calling. You're a comedian," she chuckled.

After that, practically all of their conversations started and ended with a joke. Naomi-Ruth enjoyed Dexter's sense of humor. Her dad had been the same way with Vera. He was the complete opposite of who he was in the pulpit. Her parents used to stay up until the wee hours of the morning, laughing and cracking jokes. Naomi-Ruth admired their bond and yearned for it for herself.

When Pastor Lewis asked for her hand in marriage, Naomi-Ruth presumed she was getting the type of love from a man as her mom had enjoyed in her dad. On her mini-moon, Dexter had reminded Naomi-Ruth that her parents hadn't courted the traditional way. They had busied themselves with the work of the Lord, and it had strengthened their bond in becoming man and wife. Dexter had said that was the best courtship there was, and it would be the foundation of their marriage. It had slipped Naomi-Ruth's mind, but she did follow in Vera's footsteps.

Did I marry my dad's clone? Her lips quivered.

However, she didn't recall her father dictating what her mom wore or preventing her from having a job. The more Naomi-Ruth thought about it, the more it dawned her that her mom had always worn dresses and never had a job. And up until her rape, Naomi-Ruth had only been allowed to wear dresses. Levi and Vera had finally granted her permission to include pants in her wardrobe after Naomi-Ruth had fussed that skirts might cause more problems.

What have I done?

Chapter Fourteen

Pray Until Something Happens . . .

Naomi-Ruth's mind swirled with confusion. She couldn't seem to grasp one thought before another took its place. Heading to Desirae and Rosalind's home, she hoped her friend could give her some clarity. They hadn't spoken since Dez had left Naomi-Ruth's wedding in tears. Nothing was adding up to her, and it caused Naomi-Ruth to question herself and what God wanted for her life. She knew that every marriage had its difficulties. However, they hadn't gotten up or out of bed fully after getting to know each other intimately before things had turned.

The way Dexter had catered to her body, kissing and caressing her, was how Naomi-Ruth had envisioned it would be like when she gave herself to a husband for the first time. She'd had no real contact with a man before or after the rape. Naomi-Ruth had vowed to save herself for marriage. Nothing was making sense to her. The more she reflected on it, the harder she pushed the gas pedal. Before she realized it, she was in front of Desirae and Rosalind's complex. It was the same place that Naomi-Ruth had restored her friendship with Dez. They had remained in that home since moving from next door to the Pattersons. Desirae had purchased the condo for Rosalind for her sixty-fifth birthday. Rosalind said she would only accept it if Desirae agreed to stay there with her until she started her own family.

Naomi-Ruth jumped out of the car and rushed to the door. As the door opened, she lost it.

"Dez, I don't know what to do. He . . . He wants me to end it all," she bawled.

"Nomi, you are not making sense. Please try to catch your breath. Who wants you to do what?"

"Dexter does. He was a whole other person this morning. I don't know who the man I woke up to this morning is."

"Nomi, real talk, you didn't know the man you married or went to bed with either. I am sorry, but I have to be honest."

"That's not true, Dez. From the wedding until the honeymoon, he was the same as he had always been with me. He was cracking jokes and making me blush. He made me feel like I was the only woman in the world. And that was just by the way he looked at me."

"I understand all of that, but there is a person attached to the things he made you feel. You didn't take the time to get to *know* him."

"My mom and dad married without dating the conventional way, and they were together for over fifty years."

"And I am sure both of them experienced everything you are feeling right now. I felt there was so much more to Pastor Lewis that you needed to get to know before you two married. He's not Pastor Patterson. Your dad was different."

"They are alike in so many ways, which is what attracted me to Dexter."

"They are also different in many ways too. You don't marry off attraction. Look what I went through. You should've used my mistake as a lesson. Nomi, he didn't let you plan your wedding. Your mom left you the wedding dress that she'd made, hoping you would wear it to your wedding because she knew she wouldn't be there physically. She planned her wedding because Pastor Patterson allowed her to. As I said, they are two completely different men. All of it eats me up so badly. I pray you're ready because I can see it as clear as day. Pastor Lewis is about to take you for a ride."

"You know he wrote a letter saying I had to end my friendship with you, and before that, he said he wanted me to work in ministry full time and to dress like Mother Diane."

"Is that what you were trying to say? Wait. He said to close the boutique, and his exact words were he wants you to dress like Mother Diane?" She laughed.

"What's so funny? I don't understand how any of this is amusing. This is serious, Dez."

"First, I just finished telling Mom that I wouldn't be shocked if you would have to choose between Pastor and me. Mom grinned and said I was insane. I guess I was prophetic. Second, you can't work and have to dress like the mothers of the church. That's nuts."

"Well, I am *not* choosing. You're not just my friend. You're my *sister*. I can't believe that's what you thought."

"Pastor Lewis has some serious control issues. He has to make every decision like the color the choir should wear on Sunday. The pastor is at every committee meeting from the youth to the singles' ministry. He can attend, but the auxiliary leaders have no input any longer. Everything is done *his* way. Pastor Lewis has taken the joy out of a lot of things in that church. Why do you think half of the members left? Please don't allow him to take the joy out of your life, Nomi."

"I won't. I will go back to the house and talk to him."

"All right, Nomi. You know I'm here when you need me. I love you, and there's nothing he or you can do about it."

"I love you too, Dez."

**

The entire drive back, Naomi-Ruth's mind kicked and flipped. She hated confrontation and had never been good at it. But to give up everything she's developed from her bond with Dez to her business was something she couldn't allow to be wiped out or taken from her. At this time, Naomi-Ruth missed her parents. Whenever matters became overpowering, they always knew what to do.

What would Mom and Dad tell me to do? she wondered.

Stepping out of the car, Naomi-Ruth heard her papa's voice loud and straightforward, and it made her sob.

"Pray. Don't take it out of God's hands by meddling in His business. Pray until something takes place. Change has to take place when prayer is involved."

It was a message Pastor Patterson had taught and disciplined his flock and household with as far back as Naomi-Ruth could remember.

"There's my dear bride. I was troubled when you didn't acknowledge my calls," Dexter greeted her as the door opened.

"My phone was in the truck."

"Weren't you in the truck with it? Where were you?"

"No, Dexter, I wasn't in the truck with it. I stepped out of it for a minute."

"Are you all right? You look like you've been crying, and your tone sounds as if something is upsetting you."

"I apologize if I sound that way because that's not how I aimed to come off. Can we talk?"

"I thought that's what we were doing, beautiful. What's troubling you?"

"Maybe we should pray before we talk. Would that be all right with you?"

"Absolutely."

Naomi-Ruth knew soliciting God first would assist in her being capable of discussing all that was scaring her. And if Levi hadn't taught her anything else, he'd shown her how to get a prayer through.

Taking her husband by the hand, they begin to pray at the same time.

"I apologize, Dexter. Would it be all right if I prayed for us?"

"Being the head of this house and because you're upset, I think it'd be best if I led us in prayer. The Bible tells us to be quick to listen and slow to talk because anger does not produce the righteousness that God desires."

"Dexter, I am not angry. I am hurt, afraid, and unsure."

"God isn't the author of confusion, my beloved Ruth."

"He isn't, and I am not angry." She breathed deeply and exhaled before continuing. "I went to see Dez, and I also thought about all that you're expecting me to comply with."

"I am certain that it was hard for you to do, but what God has for us is for us. We cannot allow any weapon the devil has formed against us to prosper, especially if we can see it as it's forming."

"Please tell me you're not referring to Dez as the devil."

"I am not saying she is the devil, but he has used her and will continue to use anyone who will allow him to use them."

"That is a horrible thing to say. Dez isn't allowing the devil to use her to do anything. She's been through a lot and doesn't want to see me go through any of what she's encountered. I'm not saying that will happen, but we rushed into this marriage. I was all right with it and blown away by it all, but what bothers me are your expectations for me to become someone I am not."

"I know who you are. God showed you to me in a dream way before I met you. You had on a yellow and black hat with a broach made of sequins on it. Your suit was the same color as your hat. But what stuck out most was that angelic face of yours."

"Are you sure that was *me* you saw? I don't wear hats, and I don't like them."

"Ruth, God doesn't make mistakes. He has ordained this marriage. He allowed me to find you so I could assist with taking you to your next level in Him. You don't like hats, but I bet you will learn to love them. I was taught these things in the Bible, and the young ladies did so while I was growing up. Ladies are to keep their heads covered, especially on Sundays."

"All I ask is that you allow me to be myself. My friendship with Dez cannot end, and I can't change my entire wardrobe or dismantle N&D's Boutique. Please give me time to show you that none of it will interfere with me being available for ministry or my responsibilities as your wife."

"I've already spoken, Ruth. I will give you time, but what I've decided was never up for debate. What I will do is give you time to complete things."

"This isn't fair, Dexter."

"What's right never seems fair, but it's always necessary."

Unable to accept another word, Naomi-Ruth raced upstairs to the bedroom, locked the door behind her, and broke down. She hadn't grieved this hard since her parents' back-to-back deaths. She had hoped to follow in Vera's footsteps and marry a God-fearing man like her dad. Dexter was that. He had taken over the church and became the new and youthful Pastor Patterson. It all had seemed right. None of what had transpired was making sense, however. Dexter used the scriptures to show Naomi-Ruth *he* was in the will of God. It was hard to digest. God isn't the author of confusion, yet she was more confused than she had ever been. What was supposed to be the happiest time of her life appeared to be turning into a nightmare.

As Dexter knocked on the door for entrance, Naomi-Ruth silently petitioned her Heavenly Father. "Dear Lord, I seek to be clear-minded in this time of distress and confusion. Father, I pray that you would give me increasing clarity of thought in my home and this marriage. Please widen the views of my understanding and grant me true wisdom. I'm weary and need you. I need your strength. Your Word says your joy is my strength. This pressure is backing me into a corner, making me powerless. I need your strength and direction. I am nothing without you and cannot do any of this without you. Help me to see what your plan is for my life and this union. God, I call on you for your protection and your direction in my life. Please forgive me if I moved too quickly without consulting you. Help me see your hand in this marriage and give me peace to move forward. In Jesus' name, I pray. Amen."

Chapter Fifteen

Dream Come True . . .

Dexter had allowed Naomi-Ruth to mature and blossom in the Lord before he made his move to ask for her hand in marriage and wed her. He had watched her stand in the background before and after the deaths of Pastor Patterson and Vera. She had instructed everyone on the concerns of her father's dying wishes for the staff and auxiliary heads of the church without being in the center of attention. From Pastor Lewis's observations, Naomi-Ruth had avoided being seen or heard. Her shyness was attractive to Dexter. However, to become the first lady, his wife, Naomi-Ruth needed to be comfortable with being a prime focus. Whenever he attended the auxiliary meetings, he would take charge and almost always include a view or opinion from Naomi-Ruth. He had told G-ma Dye it was his way of grooming his wife for her calling.

Over time, Naomi-Ruth began to break out of her shell. She spoke without an invitation in a discussion and took over as the choir director when Mia's, the appointed director, pregnancy had restricted her tasks. That gesture caused Dexter to recognize she was ready. He'd purchased Naomi-Ruth's dress and the engagement and wedding rings after his initial discussion with Pastor Patterson. Dexter thanked God Naomi-Ruth's weight hadn't increased since meeting her three years ago.

Pastor Lewis had given G-ma Dye and her team the ceremony's details the day after he'd presided over Pastor Patterson's home going service. The time of Levi's illness was an improper time to ask for his daughter's hand in marriage again, but Mother Diane had disagreed and felt Dexter should solicit Levi's blessings.

"Dexter, don't you think you should go down to the nursing home and talk to Pastor?"

"Not while he is on his deathbed. That would be selfish of me to do something like that. Besides, I already asked him, G-ma Dye."

"And he didn't give you an answer. He told you to come back when you were sure."

"He didn't say no, either. That only tells me he wanted to make sure I was who Bishop Livingston had described me to be. He saw it, which is why out of all of the clergy in the church, he left his congregation to me. God showed me my wife, and Ruth is her, G-ma Dye. I don't need Pastor's blessing again because he indirectly gave it to me already, and above all, my God blesses the union. That alone is enough for me."

"You owe it to him out of respect to receive his blessing, Dexter. I understand what you're saying, but God does things in decency and order. Getting Pastor's blessing is divinely required."

G-ma Dye's comments cut Dexter deeply. However, when he eventually decided to go and talk to Pastor Patterson, he was notified of Levi's passing. That pushed the proposal, wedding, and everything back. Pastor Lewis believed God that the right time would present itself for him to propose to Naomi-Ruth after that. He was prepared because he wanted the day to be one to remember whenever the occasion would take place. It just so happened that on the Sunday of their wedding, the lead singer's son had come down with a stomach bug, preventing her from attending service. Unbeknownst to Pastor Lewis or the congregation, Naomi-Ruth would fill in. They'd heard her sing before, but she'd never taken over and led a song under the anointing of God the way that she had that morning. At that hour, he recognized it was time and shifted the topic and scriptures for his sermon. That was G-ma Dye and her staff's cue to prepare for a wedding.

Everything had gone better than Pastor Lewis had expected. The only thing that'd bothered him was Pop Reg not witnessing his union. While driving home from service seven years ago, Pop Reg had fallen asleep at the steering wheel and lost his life. Dexter wished he were alive to see him marry the woman of his dreams to prove Pop Reg wrong. After losing his and Tamariane's son, Dexter devoted everything to maintaining, preaching, and abiding by the Word of God. If a female looked in his direction, it was as if she were invisible. Dexter didn't allow himself to see it or entertain anything that wasn't uplifting to his spirit. Women weren't what he sought after in that season of his life. Pop Reg teased him as he always did whenever he'd notice a young lady showing Dexter interest, and he refused her advances.

"Boy, let me ask you something."
"What is it, Pop Reg?"
"What happened to you after Tamariane? Do you like women anymore?"
"What kind of question is that?"

"A question you're avoiding. Please don't tell me you're into men now."

"Pop Reg, the Lord showered down burning sulfur on Sodom and Gomorrah and destroyed them. Do you honestly think I would allow myself to fall from God's grace again? He created men and women to be together, not men and men or woman and woman."

"And you're raining down scriptures and dodging my question. Is this your way of coming out of the closet? If so, get back in it. I don't think I can deal with you being so heavenly minded and gay at the same time. It's too much for an old man to carry."

"That's sick. Can I be concerned about myself and making it to heaven right now without you passing judgment?"

"I bet not catch you in Dye's bras and wigs, or I'm putting you out."

"God showed me my wife in a dream, but I haven't met her yet. That's why I don't pay any mind to the females that come at me."

"Lord, I hope it isn't one of those men that dress up like women."

Anytime they were alone, their discussions resulted in Pop Reg questioning Dexter's masculinity. Dexter knew he was mocking him and didn't mean it. He just wished Pop Reg could see and meet the wife of his dreams. Naomi-Ruth was who he saw in his thoughts in his early twenties. The same woman was crying in his master suite now. He didn't enjoy seeing or hearing Naomi-Ruth cry. When they first got married, Pastor Lewis knew things would be rough in the beginning, but he'd never expected the tears. Although marriage, getting to know each other, and living under the same roof was new and would be a time of testing, he didn't want to see it. Dexter believed there was nothing too hard for God. He had done everything the right way in the sight of the Lord this time. Therefore, everything involving their household and union would be blessed.

No matter what was going on between the two of them, Dexter knew God covered them. He didn't make mistakes, but man did. Pastor Lewis had waited to wed before he exposed his affection for his beloved Ruth. Dexter's dreams embodied before him the day he came face-to-face with Naomi-Ruth. A craving for her festered inside of him. Pastor Lewis desired Sister Naomi in every way possible. Intellectually, physically, personally, and spiritually. He hadn't ever encountered this type of passion for a woman before. The more time Dexter spent near or around Naomi-Ruth, the higher his craving for her rose, which is why he'd waited before having her until after they married. Pastor Lewis had chosen to prove himself, and more importantly, God, that his love for Naomi-Ruth surpassed sex. Naomi-Ruth's insecurities peaked when Dexter had recommended that they not rush into intimacy.

As they entered the room for the first time as man and wife, Naomi-Ruth allowed Dexter to get comfortable as she freshened up in the bathroom. Mother Diane's assistant had given Naomi-Ruth a sheer, lace, floral, baby-doll negligée with sheer cups and matching G-string panties. After making her way out of the bathroom, Dexter's eyes trace Naomi-Ruth's delicate beauty. She was the vision of the sacred beauty of the wife and companion he desired her to be.

"Wow, you are breathtaking."

"Thank you, Pastor, I mean Dexter. I just want my first time and our first time together to be enchanting."

"I am not your pastor right now. I am your husband."

"My apologies, Dexter. I want this to be special for both of us."

"Everything about you, including our pledge to each other, is extraordinary. But first things first. I want you to come over here and talk with me for a minute."

"Don't you think we should save the talking for later?" She winked her eye.

"I'm going to love coming home to you."

"I promise not to let you down." She took a seat next to him.

"I know you won't, beautiful. I know this is our wedding night, and right now, we should be all over each other, but I want to wait and absorb your beauty before we take part in each other."

"Dexter, that's not making too much sense. Do I not turn you on? Am I no longer attractive to you? Do you prefer me better with clothes on? I don't understand why you don't want me when you can have me. I am your wife."

"My beloved Ruth, I want you in every way possible. In fact, now that you're mine, I have permission to have you whenever I want you."

"You just don't want me now, is that what you're saying?"

"That is not what I said. The right moment will present itself. Our bodies will lead us. We don't have to rush intimacy. I want this to be right. Today was everything I dreamt it would be. Let's bask in the ambiance of it all."

Naomi-Ruth locked herself in the bedroom for over two hours, and Dexter's concern grew. Instead of knocking on the door again, he used his key to gain entrance. His wife had fallen asleep across the bed, making him smile in adoration. She was a picture of beauty that only God could have crafted. Once in arm's distance, he reached and lifted Naomi-Ruth from the bed and cradled her as if she were a newborn. Her eyes widened, realizing she wasn't dreaming.

"Dexter, what are you doing? Please put me down."

"Not until you tell me you forgive me."

"What do I forgive you for, Dexter?"

"Misunderstanding me."

"What did I misunderstand?"

"Everything I've done and asked wasn't out of malice. I love you and have since I saw you in my dreams. We belong together and will have to sacrifice some things for better things to come into materialization."

"Why is it that I am the only one being asked to give things up and change?"

"What would you like me to change?"

"I would like you to give me a chance to figure things out for myself. If things don't work out, and I have to make some adjustments, allow me to see it and do it. Our lives transformed in less than a week, and you're expecting me to overlook everything that means a lot to me. The reason I have N&D's Boutique is that my dad believed in me. That is all I have left that he's gifted me. You have to see how much the boutique means to me. I've been through more than you're aware of, and my passion for fashion saved my life by the grace of God when I wanted to end my life. And do you know who God allowed to be in my life to help me through it all? It was Desirae and Rosalind."

"I hear everything you're saying, but the Bible instructs me to love you the way Christ loves the church, and I will do just that. And as your husband and the man of this house, you have to follow my lead. You cannot follow me unless you love me more than your own life, and that includes everything and everyone you've mentioned. And to correct you, you still have the church. It's in our name."

"You hear me, but you're not listening to me, Dexter. You keep trying to confuse me with the scriptures."

"There is no confusion. The Word is right all by itself. I am listening to everything you're saying and will give you time, Ruth. Now, can we kiss and make up?"

Naomi-Ruth blushed in response. Dexter placed her on the bed and hovered over her a minute before dipping his head to kiss her. His heart beat with nervous jitters when he rose and met her eyes. When he realized she was nervous too, it caused him to want to treat her like fragile porcelain. He slid the straps of her lingerie down to reveal her firm, tipped breasts. Unable to contain his composure any longer, Dexter became one with his wife over and over throughout the night.

Chapter Sixteen

Those Feelings Again . . .

At 30, Desirae remained a virgin. She wondered if she would end up dying without experiencing love, marriage, and intimacy. After Garrett, Desirae devoted her time outside of working at the boutique to taking care of herself, which included therapy and attending service with Rosalind. Desirae saw a change in Rosalind, such as her rolling in euphoria. Desirae wanted whatever her mom was on. Rosalind attributed her state of mind to spending time in the presence of God.

Desirae thought Rosalind was holding off flipping out on her because she was thankful to have her baby girl back home. And Rosalind didn't want to cause any friction between them because she was worried that Dez would take off again. However, that was the last thing Desirae thought about doing. Dez realized Rosalind's 180 when she finally opened up to her. Rosalind repeatedly said what was required of her to speak to her child as a mother. She never talked about her childhood other than her mother had had a sick passion for alcohol. Later, she'd cover it up, saying life comes at you with the good, the bad, and the ugly, and it is up to the person on how they would respond and deal with those matters because God would not put more on us than we could bear.

***

"Dez, you can't continue beating yourself up. You cannot allow this situation to drown you. There's so much life for you to live and experience. We all make mistakes, but we are changed by them, hopefully, for the better. Everything is going to be all right. You need to pray and talk to God more."

"Mom, you sound like Pastor Patterson. We left because he preferred to pray, and now, you're saying that's what I need to do?"

"Princess, I was so wrong about that one. Although I still don't agree with how Pastor Patterson went about it, I now realize praying was the best thing for all of us, especially Nomi. Our prayers can reach places that we cannot physically go."

"Wow, I was gone for six months and come home to a praying mother."

"I wish I had known then about praying and turning things over to God a long time ago. I was so headstrong. I refused to allow myself to go there. Had I done that then, I would not have wandered around bitter and angry with everything and everyone for so long. And I wouldn't have been living a complete lie either."

"What are you talking about, Mom?"

"For years, I didn't work. I pretended to go to work when, in actuality, I was volunteering at the nursing home I now work for."

"Mom, have you been sipping on the communion juice? None of what you're saying is making any sense at all. We had food, a car, and a roof over our heads. If I am not mistaken, it's impossible to have or keep any of those things without an income. How were you able to do any of that if you were unemployed?"

"I had my 401(k) for a while and government assistance to cover up my lie."

"Wait. So, we were on welfare? Why, when there wasn't anything wrong with you? Mom, you could work, so why would you take from the system when you didn't need it? You drilled into me the importance of not being lazy and that I had to work and go to college if I wanted to make something of myself."

"I needed it because I couldn't work. Something happened to me, and I wasn't able to talk about it. I never dealt with it. I just put in the back of my mind and filed it away," Rosalind explained.

"Mom, what are you saying to me right now? What happened to you?"

"When you left, the feelings of loneliness, embarrassment, hopelessness, and anger resurfaced in an unusual way. I believe it was because I didn't have you here to occupy my mind. Too much time on my hands allowed me to think, pushing me to the verge of a nervous breakdown. Fear pushed me to seek help, and I sought a therapist. She helped me face the nightmare I've been trying not to go to sleep and face for all of those years."

"Nightmare? What?"

"Dez, while at work almost ten years ago, I . . . I was raped and fired because of it."

"Mom, how can they fire you when someone hurts you? We need to sue someone. They have to pay!"

"Long story short, my rapist was the head boss's son, so they found a loophole to get rid of me to hide what he did to me."

Outside of counseling, this was the first time Rosalind had admitted to being raped out loud.

"I am so sorry, Mom. How could someone do that to you? Oh my God! Now, I know why you said you knew there was something more going on when Nomi was hurt. Why didn't I see that? I love you so much, Mom. I am sorry. We'll get through this together," Desirae sobbed.

"Baby girl, I'm in a much better place emotionally now. I was so stuck in my head that I allowed it to affect every area of my life negatively, but by the grace of God, I am now free."

"I want that same freedom. I want counseling and a relationship with God to help me get out of my way. He is really helping you, Mom."

Desirae's road to recovery had her feeling good about the direction her life was going. Therapy helped her see the mistakes she'd made in her relationships. Her attraction to Garrett had been normal, but her mistake was thinking she had to be a wife to give her heart to a man. She'd taken dating and getting to know Garrett out of the equation. Vera and Pastor Patterson had always taught Desirae and Naomi-Ruth that the Bible commanded them not to have sex or give themselves to a man before marriage. They said the only way God would approve of sexual relationships is if it were between a man and his wife. Desirae had taken this teaching to heart. Hence, that was why she'd felt she needed to marry Garrett before they could officially date and have sex. Discussing her beliefs with her therapist had helped her see marriage wasn't the problem. It was hopefully an end result. The problem was not getting to know herself or Garrett before she accepted his proposal and married him. Desirae now knew she could date and give her heart to a man without walking down the aisle first. What she vowed to do is hold out on sexual relations until the right man found her. Even at the age of 30, she still stood on this belief.

After that session, Desirae felt a burden lift off of her. She'd been angry with herself for quite some time. Rosalind was elated to learn Dez's mind was in the right place. They'd had a disagreement a few weeks before her session.

"Dez, I just met your husband." Rosalind burst through the door.

"Mom, are you serious right now? I am not getting married again. I tried it, and it's not for me."

"Keep talking to your therapist, and she'll help you change your mind. In the meantime, I need you to make sure you're extra dazzling for church Sunday because I invited him to service."

"I am ignoring you right now. I dress fine, and I will not go out of my way for him or any other man. Besides, I am not interested."

"For now, you may not be interested, but that will change. You'll see."

"Goodbye, Mom. I'm going to my session."

Sunday arrived. Desirae caught a flat tire and made it to church right before the choir marched into the sanctuary. As she made her way to the choir stand, Desirae caught a glimpse of Rosalind grinning like a schoolgirl. Once in the choir stand, she realized why her mom was showing all of her pearly whites as she eyeballed the five foot eleven, broad-shouldered, cocoa-chocolate man standing next to Rosalind. From where she was, the same emotions she felt for Garrett suddenly consumed her. Apprehensive about where her mind was taking her, Desirae brushed the feeling off, avoided Rosalind and her guest at all costs, and waited to explain how she was feeling to her therapist at her next session.

Much to her surprise, Desirae ran into Rosalind's mystery guest she'd shied away from that morning at church at an open therapy session. The guest appointed to speak on emotional well-being was the assistant pastor of a Full Gospel Assembly in Raleigh, North Carolina. During the session, Desirae went from falling over her words to becoming silent. Dez did her best to avoid any further eye contact. She thought she had slipped under the same spell she'd fallen under with Garrett. But it was a whole other level. Running into him again now had her feeling the same pull, and the nerves returned. The mystery man was Xavier Washington.

No matter how fast she sought to break toward the door at the end of the session, her legs couldn't keep up with how fast her mind was going. Arriving at the exit, Mr. Washington stopped Desirae by standing in the doorway. He was blocking her exit.

"I believe I know you from someplace, don't I?" Xavier grinned.

"No, I think you might be confusing me for someone else."

"No, I never forget a face. I'm bad with names, for certain, but I don't forget faces, especially not my future bride's face."

"Umm, sir, you're obviously mistaking me for someone else. I can guarantee you I am not who you think I am."

"Yes, I know who you are. But I might have come off the wrong way and too straightforward, so let's start over." Xavier cleared his throat and extended his hand. "Hello, I am Xavier Washington and am visiting New York for the first time on business. I was wondering if you'd like to do me the honor of treating me to some Starbucks. Then you can tell me all there is to know about The Big Apple."

"What?" Desirae broke out in amusement.

"See? I knew I'd get a smile and not that tough exterior for too long. Now, if you don't mind, please lead the way to my coffee." He backed out of the doorway.

Desirae's mind said no, but her heart turned against her. "That might have been the funniest thing I've ever heard. Since I am going in that direction, I can point you to the closest Starbucks."

"I'm sure you meant you'll escort me to the place where we'll sit and sip java together."

Shaking her head, Desirae led the way, expressionless. Xavier skipped alongside her like a schoolboy mocking her.

"I can point you in the direction because I'm tough now. Move out of my way." He trotted along.

"I did not say that," she giggled.

"You've been smiling a lot, so I think I will call you 'Giggles.'"

Although she didn't have a problem speaking up for herself and loved the person that looked back at her in the mirror every day, something about Xavier made her nervous. She found being around him caused butterflies to flutter in her belly. Her palms were sweaty, and she could not avoid the schoolgirl giggling. As they approached Starbucks, Desirae's heart skipped a beat. Her mind told her to keep walking, but the tugging at her heart pushed her through the door.

"Since I am not a coffee drinker, you can order whatever you want first. I'll have a Chai tea latte."

"Believe it or not, I've never had a cup of coffee in my life. I thought that was what New Yorkers do since there are so many coffee shops everywhere. There isn't this many in North Carolina."

"Wait a minute. You don't drink coffee?"

"Nope. I just thought it'd be cool for my new friend to treat me to something to drink."

"You're completely insane."

"Thank heaven. God has my mind because I'd be even more of a mess if He didn't," he snickered.

After laughing together, Desirae and Xavier found a table in a corner and talked as if they've known each other forever. The more Xavier spoke, the more comfortable he made Desirae feel. While talking, she learned his grandma Minnie raised him, and Xavier's mom was on drugs and turned to prostitution to feed her habit. She had left Xavier in the hospital during the night and never returned. Grandma Minnie took him in and raised him, teaching him to love his mother, Carolyn, no matter what. Xavier wasn't raised in the church. He'd come to the Lord three years before meeting Desirae. It had been eight months since they ordained him as a minister. Mr. Washington was single, and outside of a kiss to the lips, he hadn't ever been intimate with a woman before.

He had met Rosalind in the grocery store. She was humming a hymn his grandma used to sing all of the time. He just had to say something to her and find out what church she attended. Between talking about her church and giving the address, Rosalind spoke highly about her daughter and even showed him pictures of Desirae. The color left Desirae's face after noticing Xavier was using it as another opportunity to poke fun at her.

"You were a cute little, chunky baby."

"Oh my goodness, stop." She shielded her face behind her hands.

"Aww, look at you, Giggles. You know I never saw a recent picture of you, right?"

"How did you know who I was then?"

"I didn't need to see any recent pictures to know who you were. I saw you in the choir stand and carried you back to my hotel with me in my prayers. And God brought you to my session."

"That is crazy, but I don't want to lead you on. I am not ready for a relationship."

"I am just looking to be your friend right now—nothing more, nothing less. I know where this will end up, and I don't want to go there without you becoming my friend first."

Once again, Xavier left Desirae speechless. He couldn't be any more perfect in her eyes after hearing he's saving himself for marriage. His life and who he shared a bed with were vital to him. Finding God solidified everything his grandma had taught him to believe. She wasn't a churchgoer, but Grandma Minnie had said she'd attended religiously in the past. She realized a relationship with God was more important. Grandma Minnie was the reason Xavier believed how he did. Desirae almost fell out of her chair listening to him, because she'd never before heard a man of God talk and think like him. It was all too good to be true.

"Can I ask you a question?"

"Sure. Fire away."

"You said your grandma used to attend church, but she felt a relationship with God was more important."

"You know I asked her the same question in a million different ways because it made little sense to me. I didn't think there was a difference. I thought Grandma was using it as an excuse because she preferred to stay home to listen and watch preachers on the television in her favorite chair. But one day, she broke it down to me, using the story of Mary and Martha. I'll tell you what I got from the conversation and what I live my life by. Martha ran around, engaging herself with cooking, cleaning, and preparing. There's nothing wrong with any of that. However, sometimes, we get so caught up with all the busywork like choir rehearsal, this function, that service, planning dinners, committee meetings, and everything else, that it becomes a routine. Essentially, a part of our routine is made up of many tasks. We're so caught up doing that we're not taking in. Mary sat at Jesus' feet to learn and get to know Him better. I am not saying that one cannot do the work of the Lord, but sometimes, we get so caught up in all of the work that we become self-righteous in our religious works. Hence, the judgment and fights for titles and a position instead of having a relationship with the Lord like Mary. For instance, in any relationship, to get to know each other, it requires spending intimate time with the other person. If you're busy working, how can you have quality time for Jesus when He's in your presence?"

"You just said a mouthful, Xavier. I never wanted to do too much because I enjoy spending time with my mom, working at the boutique, and spending time alone. Mom and I play Bible trivia. I've learned so much like I used to in Sunday school. Now, you're making me reexamine all I do because I don't want to become too busy having Jesus sitting around waiting for me. It makes me think about the song 'He Was There All the Time.' Mom sings it often."

"That's it right there."

Desirae and Xavier chatted for hours, entertaining each other through dinner. Xavier had an early flight back home the following morning. He and Desirae exchanged numbers, vowing to spend all the time they could to develop a solid friendship. Desirae couldn't wait to call Naomi-Ruth to tell her all about Mr. Washington. And she knew Rosalind would drive her insane about it when she found out. Either way, Desirae was thrilled about getting to know Xavier. Everything about him differed from any of the men she had crossed paths with, specifically men in the church.

Chapter Seventeen

Let It Go . . .

It was their first Sunday returning to the church as husband and wife. Naomi-Ruth was on cloud nine after spending the balance of the week and weekend honeymooning with Dexter. She was feeling extra good because Pastor Lewis didn't burden her about her attire or her relationship with Desirae. There wasn't any mention of either subject after their last disagreement.

As Pastor Lewis took his bride by the hand, escorting her to the first pew where her mom used to sit, Naomi-Ruth beamed as she thought victoriously, *Maybe, I got through to him, and he will see things differently. It's just a matter of time.*

After she took her seat, Pastor Lewis headed to the pulpit as the choir ministered to the congregation. Once on the podium, the choir turned the service over to Dexter.

"It feels good to be back in my Father's house. God surely has been good to me."

"I'm sure he has. Ain't God good?" the flock returned.

"I want to get straight to the Word this morning. The Lord gave me something for you this morning. Turn with me in your Bible to Ecclesiastes 3:6. We're going to do something different this morning. I am going to ask you to stand and read with me."

"A time to get, and a time to lose; a time to keep, and a time to cast away," the church read in unison.

"Before taking your seats, turn to your neighbor and tell that person, I don't know about you, but I am letting it all go," Pastor Lewis directed, and the congregation obeyed. "If I were to use a topic this morning, it would be 'Let it go.' Church, just because people had the approval to walk with you yesterday, it doesn't mean they'll have the same privilege to walk with you today. Sometimes, you have to get out, not just for yourself but for the individuals you're connected to. Let it go for what's locked up inside of you. Let it go. Leave the comfortable and the familiar. It might be uncomfortable for the moment, and weeping may endure for a night. However, joy will come in the morning. What you're cleaving to is locking up your joy. Your destiny, your marriage, and your happiness are all imprisoned by what you're holding on to. People of God, let it go," Pastor Lewis concluded.

Naomi-Ruth's muscles tensed throughout the sermon. Her heart shred listening to Dexter use the pulpit to address the disagreement they'd had. Service could not have ended fast enough. Naomi-Ruth couldn't hold back the tears during the benediction. She turned and stalked out of the sanctuary. Desirae saw the heartache in Naomi-Ruth's face as she went by and rushed out after her. She caught up with her before Naomi-Ruth could make it to her car.

"Nomi, what's wrong? You can't leave out of the service like that without greeting the people. You're the first lady now."

"I am not in good enough spirits to talk to anyone today, Dez."

"You know your husband will have a fit. Does he know you're leaving like this?"

"Honestly, I don't care what he knows right now. I need time to myself. It's all too much for me at the moment," she sniffled.

"What's the matter, Nomi?" Dez pulled her into an embrace.

"I don't want to talk about it here. I'm going to my parents' house. Can you take me there? I'm so upset that I forgot I rode in with Dexter."

Levi and Vera had left their home to Naomi-Ruth. She hadn't been back to the house since marrying Dexter. The only thing on her mind was to crawl into her old bed and cry herself to sleep. She declined to talk to Dez about what was troubling her because she required space to herself. Dexter and Pastor Lewis were two different men in Naomi-Ruth's eyes. And for the first time since Pastor Lewis had become chief pastor of her father's church, Naomi-Ruth realized she was having a hard time agreeing with him.

Without taking off her Sunday attire, Naomi-Ruth climbed into bed and sobbed violently. Memories of her parents swarmed her mind, provoking her to cry harder. For the first time since their passing, Naomi-Ruth mourned their loss. She was feeling like everything was caving in on her, and she'd lost everything, including herself. Marrying Dexter was supposed to have added to her instead of taking away from her by Pastor Lewis. Naomi-Ruth was afraid to express her thoughts out loud, which was one of the reasons why she'd asked Dez to give her time with a promise that they'd talk later. To Naomi-Ruth, Dexter was loving, passionate, funny, and he made her relaxed. Pastor Lewis, on the other hand, gave her anxiety. He wanted to isolate her. He was demanding and wanted to control every aspect of her life.

As sleep began to alleviate the nagging thoughts consuming her, Naomi-Ruth was frightened by pounding at the front door. She knew who it was by the three steady taps and pause because Dexter used that same rhythm each time. Although her mind told her to ignore him, she went to the door.

"Please, just let me rest!" she shouted from the other side of the door.

"Ruth, please, open this door. You're not going to leave your pastor . . . I mean, your *husband* standing out here like this, are you?"

"Yes, I am. I apologize, but I need time alone. Please give me some space, and we can talk another time."

"That's not an option. We have to talk *now*. I am *not* one of your friends, Naomi-Ruth. I am your *husband,* and I am asking you to open this door, please."

"I can't, Dexter. It's important for me to have some space right now. Everything happened too fast. Please give me time to clear my head."

"This is not how it's done, Ruth. You embarrassed me in church. Everyone was looking for you, and I turned around, and you were gone. I had to make up an excuse that you weren't feeling well. I am not leaving until you open this door, Ruth."

"Sorry, but I cannot open this door. I have to keep the little bit of sanity I have."

Pastor Lewis couldn't imagine going home without Naomi-Ruth by his side. He slept in the car overnight. On her way to the kitchen in search of something for a headache, Naomi-Ruth saw Dexter's car in the driveway.

Why is he still here? I guess I have to get this over with. She exhaled and opened the door and invited him in.

"Thank God it's warm out, or I would have frozen in that car."

"You could have respected my wishes and gone home, Dexter."

"And you could have stuck around to work things out. You can't run and hide at your parents' place whenever something is bothering you. Do you mind telling me what happened? What's wrong, Ruth?"

"You're not serious, are you?"

"Did I miss something, Ruth?"

"Dexter, you found a scripture in the Bible and preached an entire sermon on me letting go of my life for me to be happy. You don't recall that?"

"Ruth, it was the word God gave me for His people. It cuts and judges the hearts of the saved and unsaved. Do you really think I'd find a message to preach to the congregation about my wife?"

"It's also a two-edged sword, so while you're cutting, you should deal with your own stuff. And, yes, I do believe you wrote your sermon about me, and that's what you did. There's no way God told you to get up there and say those things. In fact, that was the fastest sermon you've ever preached. You usually expound on the Word. That's how I know God wasn't anywhere in that message. If this is how it's going to be, I want no part of this marriage. It hurts me to say this, but love doesn't hurt. You're supposed to love me the way Christ loves the church. Jesus wouldn't do me like this."

"Ruth, I will say it again. I gave my congregation what God gave to me. We vowed for better or for worse. Divorce will never be on the table. We'll be together till death parts us. You cannot throw divorce in the air and run off whenever you're emotional. We have to discuss things."

"There's no talking to you, Dexter. You use the scriptures to chastise me and validate your warped way of thinking. I've come a long way, and I am *not* a victim. I won't allow you to manipulate the Word and use it against me. My dad never treated my mom like this. You hurt me, Dexter."

"None of what you're saying is true. It will take some time, but you will see that I am nothing like what you've described. We will get through this. I just need you to come home so we can make up and fix this."

"Right now, I ask that you give me time. I am not ready to go back there. For me to be the wife you need me to be, I have to take this time to get myself together. Please allow me this space, Dexter."

"I don't believe in living separately. A man belongs with his wife. But I will give you time and space this one time only. Please don't get used to this because I refuse to go through this a third time, Ruth. So, please, get whatever it is that you need out of your system and come on home."

"What are you talking about? We haven't been together that long for this to be a second time, let alone a third time."

"It's nothing. Just do what you need to do, Ruth. I need you home." He made his way out the door.

Naomi-Ruth was proud that she stood up for herself. She was still hurting, but she had to defend herself. Marrying Dexter was one of the happiest times of her life. Surprising her and putting everything together felt good . . . at the time. Dexter was the type of man that Levi raised Naomi-Ruth to believe God had for her. Levi didn't want Naomi-Ruth to grow up and get married. He'd prefer she remained his little girl. However, after Pastor Lewis confessed that God had shown him Naomi-Ruth in a dream, Levi knew it was time to stress how he'd taught her a man was supposed to treat her.

"Ruth," Levi called her into his study.

"Yes, Papa?"

"How are things going with you?"

"Papa, why did you ask me that? What's wrong?"

"You know your father, don't you?"

"Yes, I do, and when you ask how things are going, it means something happened, or I did something wrong. So, which one is it?"

"You've been so busy with the boutique, the choir, and the singles' ministry, but are you taking any time out for yourself?"

"Papa, you're talking in circles. You know I have girls' night with Dez, and I go out with some of the women from the singles' ministry. What is this really about?"

"Are you dating anyone, Ruth? Are you thinking about it or interested in anyone?"

Naomi-Ruth couldn't help but explode in hysterics. "Oh my goodness, let me catch my breath. How hard was that for you to ask me? Your face went through so many expressions, Papa. That was hysterical."

"I'm glad you find your dad funny. But I am serious, Ruth."

"Honestly, right now, I'm not dating. I'm assuming the right man is on his way to come to find me, or you and Mom are stuck with me forever," she snickered.

"That's right, Princess. God will send the right man along. I'm sure some have already sought you, but they weren't for you. That's why you didn't notice them. I want you to remember that Christ gave up His life for the church, and that is how a husband is supposed to love you. He has to be forgiving, gentle, and patient with you. Disrespect and control don't love. I tried it with your mom, and she almost left me. Don't put up with it. Trying to control another person is the spirit of witchcraft. Remember that, Ruth. Being submissive doesn't diminish your voice. You can disagree and show honor and respect. I love you, Ruth, and I know God will send you someone like me, and when He does, you remember what I taught you. If we are like God, we have

*to love like Him. God's love is patient, kind, and peace-
ful."*
   "I will never forget, Papa."

   Thinking of the conversation she'd had with Levi
grieved Naomi-Ruth. He had prepared her for the incidents in marriage. She just hoped she didn't have to
go through it. Naomi-Ruth didn't know how long she
planned on staying at her parents' place. She just knew
it was where she desired to be at the moment. Dexter's
sermon triggered an old wound that hadn't healed. While
in the locker room when she was 14, someone took advantage of her innocence and attacked her. Naomi-Ruth
felt Dexter did the same thing. He attacked her with the
Word of God, the only source of solace that Naomi-Ruth
knew to aid her with making it into the next day.
   After Dexter left, Naomi-Ruth's thoughts ran wild,
causing her to feel paralyzed and overheated. Unable to
calm herself down, she called Dez over to help her. The
way Naomi-Ruth was feeling, she knew if she didn't relax,
she'd end up having to be rushed to the hospital for having a nervous breakdown or, God forbid, a heart attack.

Chapter Eighteen

A Grieving Spirit . . .

The last thing Dexter wanted was a division between him and Naomi-Ruth. Separation, in his eyes, created barriers, something he could not imagine being in the way of him and the love of his life. Naomi-Ruth was his wife, and they're supposed to be under the same roof. His marriage to Naomi-Ruth wasn't like the one when he was 16, and he was forced to marry Tamariane as a form of discipline. To this day, he wasn't sure how he felt about what he was forced to do back then. He and Tamariane were penalized, but at what cost? Dexter had no choice in the marriage or the scandal that resulted. If he had, he would have moved away because he didn't like how Tamarian became the talk of the church in such a negative way. This is why Pastor Lewis was so resistant to Naomi-Ruth being at her parents' house. He refused to allow anyone to speak ill toward them. Dexter's nerves got the best of him. As the man of his house, there was no reason for him to be going through the same thing. One of the primary reasons Dexter had made sure he put everything in place before asking Naomi-Ruth to marry him was so he could control how they lived. Losing Naomi-Ruth wasn't an option.

He had found his good thing, and he'd done everything according to the scriptures. How could this be taking place? God wasn't the author of a mess. Unable to calm his racing mind, Dexter asked G-ma Dye to come over because he respected her opinion. She had a way of getting through to Dexter even though sometimes, it took a little while to accept where she was coming from. Pacing back and forth, Dexter replayed the conversation he'd had with Naomi-Ruth. As he relived it, his anxiety heightened.

The vibrations of the doorbell snapped him out of his thoughts.

"Pastor," G-ma greeted as she entered.

"G-ma, you don't have to call me that. This is serious."

"You sounded serious as usual whenever it's church business."

"Not this time. Ruth left me."

"Dexter, what are you talking about? I thought you said she didn't feel well, and that's why she left immediately after service yesterday."

"She wasn't feeling *me,* so she left."

"What did you do?"

"I gave the Word as God had given it to me. Ruth thinks I preached the message concerning a disagreement she and I had."

"Son, God doesn't cause any mess. Did you use the podium to shame your bride? I was praying you wouldn't take up that habit from Bishop Livingston. You took up so many of his ways. He was an outstanding man of God, but I didn't agree with using the Word to attack or punish his wife or the people of God openly. Don't get me wrong. Some correction has to be done openly, but not every single thing."

"I disagree. Bishop did what God had instructed him to do. The Word says the Lord disciplines those whom He loves. The problem with His people is we can't stand to be corrected."

"God doesn't need you to do the disciplining for Him, Dexter. He has it under control. Don't push the people or your wife away by trying to do God's job. The Word is a two-edged sword, son. It isn't just for the receiver, but it's for the messenger as well. So, if you're expecting anyone to let something go as you preached on Sunday, then you need to begin dropping some of that weight too, son. I thought the message was a little short yesterday, but I assumed you were too busy honeymooning, so I disregarded it."

"I gave what God gave to me. Right now, this is about getting Ruth to come back home."

"You are not receiving what I'm saying or just said right now. Pray and think about the things I've said and what your wife conveyed to you and fix it. I don't want to know what your argument was about. I need you to do what you have to do to bring Naomi-Ruth home for good. Marriage isn't easy. There has to be more giving than receiving sometimes. Pop Reg and I made it as long as we did because I understood who he was, and I didn't try to change him. I didn't agree with some of the things he did, but I forgave him and continued to love him in spite of it all. If you're going to love Ruth the way Christ loves the church, you will have to sacrifice some things just like Jesus did. In this season, she needs to get to know Dexter, and you must become better acquainted with Naomi-Ruth. You're familiar with Pastor Lewis and Sister Naomi, but you know nothing about each other outside of the church setting, son. Get to know your wife . . . and Dexter too while you're at it. You've been a pastor since you were 16. Now, you have to learn how to be a man and a husband to your wife."

As the door closed behind G-ma Dye, Pastor Lewis descended to his knees. After his talk with his grandmother, Dexter was even more conflicted. He wanted his wife home now, but how could he get her home and keep the church out of his business? He knew it would take something significant to convince Naomi-Ruth to come home. The look in her eyes had told it all.

"Dear Heavenly Father, please give me clarity. Speak to me, your servant, Dexter, Lord. I'm listening. I cannot move forward without you or Ruth at home here by my side. I need my helpmate with me. I'm losing members from preaching what I know is the truth. Help me, God. My heart and mind are heavy." Tears streamed from his eyes.

"How can you lead others through their problems if you're hiding yours from them?" the Lord asked.

One thousand eight hours totaling six weeks went by, and Naomi-Ruth hadn't found her way back home. Dexter had done everything in his power to convince her things would be different. He'd apologized on many occasions and sent flowers and jewelry. He slept out in her driveway because he had to be near her, and that's as close as he could get. He even had the bathroom at her parents' place redone for her after learning there were plumbing issues. However, as it set in that Naomi-Ruth hadn't returned home in six weeks, Dexter lost it, bolting out of the truck and hammered on the front door.

"Ruth, I will not allow another second to pass by. Either I am moving in there with you, or you're coming home immediately. Now, open this door!" Dexter yelled, pounding on it.

"Please, stop all of that commotion! The neighbors will hear you again. Don't you think you've created enough scenes?" She snatched the door open.

Dexter practically lost his balance. He didn't expect her to open the door. She swore not to see him until she was ready, and it would be on her terms and not because of his outburst. The last encounter they'd had emerged after they had made love. What had appeared to have been one of the make-up sessions Dexter enjoyed had ended up driving a wedge between them.

Three weeks before after Sunday service, Naomi-Ruth had invited Dexter over for dinner. He'd been praying and fasting for things to turn around in his life. His wife was making supper, and wanting to talk answered his prayers. Naomi-Ruth had attended service as she always did and took her seat as the first lady on the front pew. Pastor Lewis asked her to continue showing her face as his wife because they had an image to uphold. Although Naomi-Ruth didn't agree with Dexter's reasoning, she'd accepted it because she knew people looked up to her, and no matter what was going on, she had to try to make things work.

Dinner was superb, and everything was made the way G-ma Dye did it. Dexter felt alive again. Naomi-Ruth prepared all of his favorite foods: macaroni and cheese, jerk chicken, sweet yams, potato salad, rolls, and peach cobbler. They conversed as they used to postmarriage, and it felt right. While helping his bride clean up after dinner, Dexter came up from behind and swept his lips against her neck. Naomi-Ruth turned to face him and tasted his lips. The heat rose as their tongues locked. Feeling the warmth of Naomi-Ruth's skin, Dexter sought to chase down the electricity sparking between them. He lifted Naomi-Ruth from her feet and brought her to the sofa. In efforts to find unity, Dexter smashed his lips into hers. As they exchanged saliva and the flames intensified, Naomi-Ruth used her forearm to nudge her husband and asked for him to give her a moment.

"Ruth, this is right. It's what we need. Just let it happen."

"I feel a little nauseated, Dexter. Give me a second to get myself together."

"I'll grab you a cup of water."

Naomi-Ruth drank the water, and they picked up where they'd left off. Dexter could not get enough of his wife. He'd missed her tremendously. Making love to her was one joy he'd looked forward to ever since they took each other's hand in marriage. As they reached nirvana, Naomi-Ruth pushed Dexter off of her and bolted to the restroom.

"What has gotten into you? Am I that much of a turn-off? You've allowed a spirit to come between us, Ruth," he shouted.

Naomi-Ruth could not respond as the wonderful spread she'd prepared splashed into the commode after erupting from her upset stomach.

"Now, I make you sick so that you're vomiting?"

Naomi-Ruth wiped her mouth and returned. "Everything *isn't* always about you, Dexter. I clearly am not well. You took a beautiful evening and ruined it. Thanks a lot."

"You were fine while making love to me. You became distracted, and some spirit made you throw up."

"Are you insane? Please gather your things and leave. I don't know what your mind is telling you, but something isn't right. I want this to work. You have to deal with the things you've hidden because you're bleeding all over the place, Dexter."

"Bleeding? What in God's name are you talking about? I knew going to some therapist wasn't a good idea for you. God is the only mighty counselor that you need. That's why you're in there pucking your brains out. Your spirit is wavering back and forth. You cannot serve two masters, Naomi-Ruth. It has to be God and Him alone. That person you're talking to isn't God. Do they even know God?"

"Dexter, I hope you're spewing this nonsense out in anger. You cannot possibly believe what you're saying.

Do you *hear* yourself? My dad used to say God was the only counselor, and on his dying bed, he and my mom realized they were wrong. You cannot cover everything up by stamping it with scripture. Sometimes, we endure things that require major surgery, but no surgery can go well without all the proper utensils available for the procedure. When some of us find salvation, we become Jesus fanatics and use God and the Word as a bandage for our deep-rooted wounds when, in actuality, we require to be cut open and then stitched back together. So, when I said you were bleeding all over the place, I was saying you have to remove the bandages and allow God to do some surgery. Counseling is doing wonders for me. I think you should go too," she sniffled.

Dexter has always had a reply, but this time, he was speechless. His beloved Ruth had said the same thing God had told him weeks ago about dealing with his problems. She'd even broken it down in a way that he's never heard before. Pastor Lewis's inner man pained even more. He left his bride at the home her parents left her and didn't speak to her until the following Sunday. Dexter was in the same position on the floor of his bedroom, crying out to God without taking a bite to eat as he did when he lost his virginity in the church basement. They were two different instances but the same crushing of his spirit.

Chapter Nineteen

The Confession . . .

Naomi-Ruth's insides had been battling her since dinner with Dexter. She regretted the entire evening because things had become uncomfortable between them because she had been feeling deathly ill since. She hadn't been able to wrap her mind around what had transpired because between nausea and vomiting, she had been sleeping every chance she got. For two weeks, Naomi-Ruth hadn't kept anything down or left the house. For the first time in her life, this would be the second Sunday in a row she'd missed church. Desirae had covered for her last week by having Rosalind ask the congregation in the morning announcements to keep First Lady Lewis in their prayers because she hadn't been feeling well. Dez reported back that Pastor Lewis cosigned when he addressed the saints and prayed for Naomi-Ruth's healing.

"Dez will have to ask Rosalind to solicit more prayers because I will not make it," Naomi-Ruth acknowledged.

Before she could shoot a text over to Dez, her stomach got queasy again, and she sprang from the bed into the bathroom. Desirae diagnosed Naomi-Ruth with food poisoning or pregnancy. Nomi believed it was a bug that wouldn't let up. She refused to entertain Dez's pregnancy theory or food poisoning.

The one thing Naomi-Ruth had enjoyed doing the past month was seeing a psychiatrist. When she finally talked to Dez and explained to her everything that had happened with Dexter, Desirae shared and recommended to her friend-turned-sister the key to her newfound peace.

"What's going on, Nomi? You've been here for almost a week now. You're a married woman. You're supposed to be with your husband."

"Dez, I cannot be there right now. That message he preached on Sunday was directed at me. It was an abuse of the pulpit and our union. He hurt me and justified it with the Word. I knew you would say I told you so, but I did not need to hear that right now."

"Wow! That was harsh. Pastor Lewis took what you two disagreed on and made a sermon out of it? Now, that is deep. But you know what? I am not surprised because Pastor Lewis is overly religious. And because of that, his relationships suffer."

"What did you say? He's religious? We all are, aren't we?"

"From what I am learning and have learned, no. The most important place for us to be is in a relationship with God. It will supersede the religious stuff. You know, the stuff that doesn't really matter. I just have a different outlook on things these days."

"Well, you're glowing like crazy, and everything you're saying makes sense. I never really looked at things in that way. Wow, where did this Dez come from?"

"My therapist recommended I go to an open therapy session. This guy Mom met in the grocery store and invited to church was the lecturer. Long story short, he and I had a long talk, and he broke down the story of Mary and Martha differently. Therapy has been doing wonders for me. I never really talked about it with you like I probably should, but I think you should try it."

"Ever since you told me you and your mom were in therapy, I have thought about going. I guess I didn't know where to start, so I left it alone."

"Well, I'll ask Xavier to recommend someone for you that specializes in emotional well-being because he lives in North Carolina. Besides, it might pose a conflict of interest eventually."

"That would be great. But back up a little bit. Who is Xavier? Why am I just learning about him? He's been to the church, you said? When did we start keeping secrets?"

"When he came to church, I ignored him and my mom. She came home talking about she had found 'my husband' and invited him to church. I stayed away from both of them that Sunday. Then I ran into him at a session. It hasn't been that long since I met him either. It was crazy."

"You stayed away from him, but knew who he was, huh?"

"That's what Mom said, but I pay attention to things, even from a distance."

"I bet you do," Nomi jested.

"We are just friends, so calm down."

"For now. I am so happy for you, Dez. Please text him now and ask him for a recommendation. I need to see the light at the end of the tunnel."

Xavier referred Naomi-Ruth to a great therapist that has allowed her to deal with the trauma she experienced as a child. Presently, the way she had been feeling emotionally, Naomi-Ruth was anxious to visit her psychiatrist. She hadn't been able to deal with or address what transpired with Dexter verbally. Her mental state seemed to be dealing with it. Along with feeling poorly lately, Naomi-Ruth had been feeling depressed and could not shake it. At first, she thought it was her body being fatigued and not wanting to do anything. But she realized that wasn't the case because she recognized the signs her therapist, Dr. Laner, had told her to look for because reliving her trauma might trigger things. Naomi-Ruth felt as if God were punishing her, and her emotional state had nothing to do with trauma because no matter what, things continued to worsen.

God, it's not supposed to be like this. I know I've made mistakes in my past, and you've forgiven me for them. But yet, I feel as if I am still paying for them, Naomi-Ruth mourned silently.

The rain spattering against the windowpane matched the tears trailing down Naomi-Ruth's face. Wishing for the calm of a peaceful night, she wanted to escape the present. She turned her thoughts inward, looking for memories that could give her peace. But tranquility could not find her.

Once inside her powder room, anxiety threatened to consume her. The area was usually transformed into the setting where she meditated and sought to reach nirvana, but now, that same space was unfamiliar and unwelcoming. Naomi-Ruth's heart was racing at an alarming rate as her stomach churned. Rubbing her sweaty palms together, she glanced in the mirror—and became blindsided by the reflection staring back at her. The image was unrecognizable and yet, so familiar. She looked as tired as she felt. Her disheveled hair, along with the dark circles beneath her blazing, golden eyes took her by surprise.

"What happened to me? Where did I go? How did I get back here?"

Tears masked her peanut butter complexion, forcing Naomi-Ruth to reflect on everything that had transpired.

"At this point in my life, there's no reason to cry over what would've, could've, or should've happened. I have to face the music," she concluded.

Taking in a deep breath, Naomi-Ruth placed the test Dez left for her on her vanity when she diagnosed her. Hesitantly, she picked it up again and opened the box. Her heart was racing, and she was slightly nauseated. With trembling hands, she administered the test. Tears welled up in her eyes. Seconds seemed like hours as she waited. She could feel the nerves as she absentmindedly bit her nails. Unable to be still, she walked back and forth, and without notice, panic struck as the indicator changed to positive.

"N-no! H-how?" she croaked. Naomi-Ruth expected the words that slipped from her lips to be a whisper, but they resounded like a reverberation throughout her master bath.

"Ruth, are you all right? Please, unlock the door," Dexter pleaded from the other side of the door.

As Naomi-Ruth watched, her hands struggled to open the door. Dexter was already pushing his way inside. She instantly became speechless as their eyes met. Confused by how he got inside the house crossed her mind, but she brushed it off, assuming she'd left the door unlocked. Her heart was hammering painfully in her chest as her breathing went from quick to next to nothing at all. In her state of numbness, the pregnancy test dropped from her hand as she bolted past Dexter, almost knocking him off balance.

"Ruth, the door was unlocked. I let myself in when you didn't answer. What's wrong? You look like you've seen a ghost." He followed behind her.

"It's bad timing, very bad timing. We can't even see eye to eye. We are separated, and a baby won't fix things, Dexter."

"What are you talking about? I said nothing about a baby. Are you saying what I think you're saying, Ruth?"

"I wish I weren't."

"Don't talk like that. In the midst of everything, God saw fit to bless us with the honor of bringing a child into the world together. It might not make sense right now because we're in the midst of it, but God knows what He's doing, Ruth."

"Dexter, you *do* know a baby cannot change things, right?"

"God is already working it out, Ruth. That is the reason I came by. Ever since our last falling out, I have been convicted. God has been dealing with me. I want you to see something. Can we play this DVD?"

"Dexter, now isn't the time to watch television."

"Please, just do this for me, Ruth."

Naomi-Ruth conceded and allowed Dexter to turn on the TV. As soon as it came on, Dexter was standing in the pulpit. He repeatedly wiped his forehead with his handkerchief and cleared his throat a few times before speaking. His lips quivered as he addressed the congregation.

"People of God, this isn't a comfortable assignment that God has me facing today, but it's necessary. It is taking me back to my childhood when I was first appointed as a youth pastor. I've made some mistakes, saints, but God has forgiven me for what I buried without dealing with it. It hurt me. Disappointment and shame controlled me for not dealing with what God was dealing with me. I submerged myself in the scriptures. Now, we know the Word of God is what leads and guides us, but what I didn't recognize then until my wife brought it to my attention is that I used these scriptures as a crutch. How can I lead you through problems when I've been hiding from my own? I am not sure if you're

aware of this, but when I was 16, I disobeyed God and lost my virginity, and as a result, the young woman became pregnant. My bishop had us do what was right in the eyes of God and marry, which troubles me today because I didn't find her how I was supposed to have, and as a result, the baby didn't make it. All of it has been a thorn in my side for all of these years. I married and divorced at 17 and have never spoken about it since. As a result, I smothered my wife and used this podium to preach away a disagreement we had. Today, I not only ask for your forgiveness. Ruth, I know you're not here today, but I am soliciting your forgiveness. I apologize for having to share this here. But this is what I have to do publicly for us to move on."

Naomi-Ruth and Dexter held each other and broke down in each other's arms. Witnessing Dexter confess his faults in humility gave her the sign she'd been praying for from God. She knew it would take time to heal and learn her spouse and vice versa, but she was willing to put in the work. This is the side of her husband she's longed to get to know, not the controlling pastor without faults.

Because things looked like they were in the process of a turnaround, Naomi-Ruth refrained from sharing her dark secret with Dexter. The only people who knew about her rape were Dez, Rosalind, and now, Naomi-Ruth's therapist. Levi and Vera took the tragedy to their graves with them.

Chapter Twenty

Nine Months Later . . . It's a Boy . . .

Things between Dexter and Naomi-Ruth was short of amazing. Because they didn't start the common way . . . love, marriage, and the happily ever after . . . Naomi-Ruth now believed God truly had been behind it all. She also agreed with Dexter. God's ways are not our ways, and sometimes, He has to shake things up so He can get the glory. Their union started rocky, but things shifted. Naomi-Ruth had to eat her words when she said a baby wouldn't fix things. The fetus growing inside of her did bring them closer together. Dexter never mentioned the boutique or her wardrobe change again. He'd even gone as far as apologizing to Desirae, which confirmed for Naomi-Ruth that her husband was the man that she knew him to be. He listened when Naomi-Ruth spoke without a critical, biblical mind-set. It's as if Dexter became human. Although he continued to preach as he always had, he was her Dexter, the man, at home.

Every time that Dexter looked at Naomi-Ruth, he became ecstatic. He was so taken up in the emotion that his speech sometimes was almost incomprehensible. Dexter would rub her belly and say things like, "Is my heir in there? Am I going to have a son?" Even before learning the sex of his unborn, Pastor Lewis was positive God would bless them with his successor. Naomi-Ruth sobbed each time he did it.

They made up for missing out on the things new couples do, such as making dinner together, having a date night once a week, and playing UNO together. Naomi-Ruth hadn't ever been to a museum, so Dexter surprised her with a three-day getaway to the Smithsonian National Museum of Natural History in Washington, D.C.

Dexter was full of surprises when Naomi-Ruth turned six months pregnant. He surprised her with a fresh start, moving into a bigger place, preparing for the baby. This gesture was mind-blowing for her. Naomi-Ruth had made herself at home when returning to Dexter's house. It just never felt like home the way it did at her parents', even with them gone. They'd spoken about looking to move into a more prominent place, but they never pushed the issue. That was . . . until after Sunday service three months earlier.

"Are we stopping somewhere before going home? You're going in the opposite direction. You should have told me because you know I'm going to need a bathroom break," Naomi-Ruth reminded him.

"Be patient, my love. I have a surprise for you."

"Please tell me what it is. It'll still be a surprise because I didn't know about it."

"That'll take the fun out of it. Don't worry, my love. We'll be there shortly."

"I cannot wait that long, Dexter. I need to know now."

"We are here, my impatient bride." He leaned over and kissed her forehead.

"My parents' house is the surprise?"

"Our home is my surprise to you."

"Our home? What are you saying, Dexter?"

"Let me help you inside so you can see for yourself."

Naomi-Ruth's eyes seemed to jump from one thing to the next. It stunned her as Dexter led her through the house, never releasing her hand.

"Do you like it?" Dexter waited until he finished the tour before asking.

He, along with Desirae and Rosalind, came together and had every room in the place renovated from traditional to contemporary. The house kept the Pattersons' charm with vintage wooden cabinets and décor.

"What? How? Oh, Dexter, this is perfect," she raved, throwing her arms around his neck.

Matters between her and Dexter were all that Naomi-Ruth could have ever dreamed of, but him surprising her by updating her childhood home for their family was more than Naomi-Ruth could ever expect. Actually, Dexter's excitement is what kept Naomi-Ruth's sanity intact. She had a love-hate affair with her pregnancy. Being able to eat whatever she wished was a dream come true to Naomi-Ruth because she didn't have to worry about her weight. Being with child gave her privilege and a reason to eat whatever she liked and gain without having to hide or drive herself crazy trying to lose it. The part she disliked was seeing the weight on her frame. Naomi-Ruth grew tremendously, putting on seventy-five pounds.

During the first trimester, there was little to no discomfort . . . only uncontrollable eating. The nausea and vomiting subsided soon after learning she was with child. At Naomi-Ruth's twentieth-week appointment, she and Dexter learned the sex of their child. Dexter's reaction to the discovery brought tears to the sonogram technician's eyes.

"First, we will go from head to toe and take a few pictures of the baby," the sono tech informed them.

Watching the monitor, Dexter boiled over in emotion. "Do you see our boy, Ruth?"

"Can you please tell us the sex? My husband will keep hinting and explode before he asks," Naomi-Ruth inquired.

The technician ran the wand over her belly and explained what she saw. "Let's see what we have."

A moment or two later, Dexter received his confirmation.

"You're correct, Mr. Lewis. It's a boy. Here is his penis between the two legs. Congratulations."

Dexter sat stunned. The rest of the sono tech's words passed over his head after learning he would have a son, a mini Dexter. He would raise his son to be godly, a warrior for the Lord. Tears left his eyes, and for one of the few times ever, he had no shame in the tears he shed.

Almost regaining his composure, Dexter slid to the edge of his chair and cried. "You're telling me my boy is in there? Does my wife have my legacy growing inside of her, ma'am? I will really have a son is what you're saying?" He pulled his handkerchief from his pocket, buried his face in it, and whimpered.

The third trimester, which Dexter referred to it as the "home spread," had him elated. He's studied every new parent, parenting, and child-birthing books he could get his hands on. Dexter was impatient with taking child-birthing classes with Naomi-Ruth. He reminded her daily about the importance of taking Lamaze classes. She, on the other hand, wouldn't mind sleeping. The insomnia Naomi-Ruth was experiencing had been a horror. Between the trips to the bathroom every five minutes, and her growing belly, it had been practically impossible for sleep to find her.

Their first class wasn't what Dexter had hoped it to be. They received handouts, learned the essentials of

Lamaze, and took part in icebreaker exercises to get to know the other expecting parents. Dexter left class dissatisfied because he thought the instructor would concentrate on the stages of labor. Eager for class, Dexter reread the material concerning breathing techniques since the instructor had informed everyone that it would be the topic they'd cover this evening.

Throughout the day, Naomi-Ruth experienced some discomfort and pressure in her abdomen. She assumes it was gas even as the pain persisted and grew stronger. All she desired was to lie down and get some rest, but Dexter would spaz out if they didn't attend tonight's class. His excitement had him taking two steps at a time as they made their way through the door. His wife's waddle slowed up a bit as the pressure increased. Realizing Naomi-Ruth wasn't by his side, Dexter turned to wait for her. As they graced the entrance, Naomi-Ruth felt the sensation of water trickling down her legs.

"Oh my goodness, Dexter. I think I peed my pants, and I can't control it."

"I can grab you a change of clothes from your hospital bag. Just stay right here for a minute, and please don't be embarrassed, Ruth. This is normal. I'm sure it's happened in this very spot over a million times."

Before Naomi-Ruth could respond, she was blindsided by an intense shooting pain to her back and lower abdomen. From the look on her face, Dexter could see the discomfort was intense this time and put two and two together.

"Ruth, this is it! You're in labor. Should I carry you to the car? Do we need an ambulance? Is there a wheelchair in this place?"

"Mr. Lewis, let's get her to the car. Do you think you're all right to drive or do you think an ambulance would be better?" the instructor questioned.

Exhaling, Dexter responded, "I can drive. Ruth, I'll bring the car up front."

The thirty-minute ride was miserable for Naomi-Ruth. The contractions left her breathless. She was in active labor and seven centimeters dilated when she reached labor and delivery. After bearing down as if she had a big bowel movement, and five pushes later, Naomi-Ruth and Dexter welcomed an eight-pound, twelve-ounce Zayvon Dexter Lewis into the world. Zayvon came out alert and peering back at his joyously sobbing parents. Naomi-Ruth and Dexter could not have prepared for this moment. All of the ups and downs they'd experienced in their lives became null and void. They could not have asked for a more perfect baby. Zayvon's tiny feet, fingers, and head full of black curls caused his parents to cry the sweetest tears. They were amazed that this little person was theirs.

"When can we take him home?" Dexter's heart pounded.

Naomi-Ruth beamed in response.

"Let's take care of first things first, Mr. Lewis. We're going to get this little guy fed and keep an eye on him and Mom overnight. If all is well, I'm sure the doctor won't have a problem with releasing them tomorrow," the nurse assured him.

Naomi-Ruth could not control the stream of tears flowing from her eyes. As Zayvon latched on for his first breast feeding, her emotions got the best of her. The person who was once inside of her and kept her up all night was now in her arms. She just wished Levi and Vera had lived long enough to meet their grandson. The more she thought about it, the harder the tears flowed. As if he read her mind, Dexter comforted his wife.

"Ruth, you are the best thing that has happened to me. If your parents were here, they would be so proud of you. I am so grateful God blessed Levi and Vera with you.

Had He not, this little blessing wouldn't be in our lives." Dexter kissed Zayvon's forehead.

G-ma Dye, Rosalind, and Desirae waited anxiously in the waiting room for the news. Each of them raced to the hospital as soon as they got off the phone with Dexter. He'd gotten so caught up that he'd forgotten they were in the lobby.

"Dexter, why don't you let everyone know Zayvon is here," Naomi-Ruth reminded him.

"Dear God, it completely slipped my mind, but I don't want to leave him yet."

"I promise he'll be right here when you return."

"You promise?" Dexter brushed his hand on the side of her face. "I love you, Ruth, and my Zay." He exited the delivery room.

Once he approached them, Dexter stretched his arms as wide as he could and tried to wrap them around all three women as they greeted him.

"He's here! My little man is as beautiful and perfect as my Ruth. She did great. We got our little boy," he whimpered.

Chapter Twenty-one

Yes or No . . .

Nothing or no one could have prepared Desirae for Nomi's pregnancy or Zayvon. She felt as if she too were expecting while Nomi was pregnant. During the times Pastor Lewis led his flock, attended church business, and while home, Dez was at Naomi-Ruth's side. Business at N&D's boutique had afforded them to employ staff, so Dez didn't have to be there as much as she used to be. It had been a blessing and a curse because whatever cravings Nomi had, Desirae experienced them with her. Rosalind said it was because they spent so much time together. They were two peas in a pod. Their waistlines agreed with Rosalind because even they expanded together. It pained Dez when she realized her clothing was clinging to her after trying on outfits to wear for one of Xavier's visits to New York.

"Nomi, everything is too small. Look at how this skirt is grabbing my backside." Dez turned her back to Naomi-Ruth.

"Well, I have some maternity pants you could probably put on. They are cute and don't really look like maternity clothes. Oh, you know. You bought most of them for me."

"This is not funny, Nomi. I am not wearing elastic pants."

"So, now the truth comes out. When I said I didn't want to be a spokesperson for the expecting moms' apparel, you swore I could get away wearing the items after I delivered because they didn't look like maternity wear. Now, those same items aren't good enough for you or Mr. Xavier, I see," she jabbed.

"And I meant what I said. That did not mean I too would look good in them. Help me, Nomi! I am freaking out."

"Did you try the emergency closet at the boutique?"

"You're a lifesaver. It completely slipped my mind."

Naomi-Ruth and Dez had a small separate closet at the boutique where they kept just emergency items. The 911 storage area contained pieces for every occasion, interview, banquet, church service, wedding, date, and funeral, if necessary. The sizes ranged from petite to curvaceous. It was a lifesaver for clients and now Desirae.

Things between Dez and Xavier had been too good to be true. At times, he'd second-guess things and self-sabotage because her feelings were getting the best of her. She was paranoid, thinking Xavier's true colors would show sooner or later. Even though she smiled at the thought of him, Desirae told herself she was not as happy as she thought she was primarily because they'd labeled their connection a friendship. In spite of it all, no matter what Dez thought or told herself, her feelings didn't agree, and neither did Xavier's. Without prompting, they daydreamed about each other. Butterflies swarmed their bellies if they knew they were going to see each other or when answering each other's calls. When Dez and Xavier were on the phone most nights, they'd fall asleep with it in their ears. Neither of them ever wanted to hang up first. At 29, they could not believe they had teenage crushes for each other.

Living in two different states was posing a conflict. It was prohibiting them from doing what their hearts yearned for—soaking up each other's air, time, and space. Since meeting, Desirae and Xavier had seen each other six times in the ten months they'd been friends. Xavier's practice had him pretty busy. Before meeting Dez, he scheduled a seven-state Emotion Health Is Wealth tour. Xavier partnered with various practices in New York, New Jersey, Connecticut, Washington, D.C., and Philadelphia to host open sessions. As a result, his time was limited. Desirae and Xavier lived by the wives' tale that communication is the foundation of every relationship. It was a staple in their blossoming companionship. Dez joked and said she talked to Xavier more than she did her mom, and they lived in the same house. But she wouldn't change it for the world, and Rosalind was beyond ecstatic. She teased Dez, threatening her not to hurt her son-in-law's feelings every chance she got. Desirae usually blushed when Rosalind threw her threats around, but Xavier being on the other end of the phone hearing it caused her to freak out.

"Dez, I picked up dinner and got extra for Nomi and Pastor. He was still at the church when I left from over that way," Rosalind shouted from the kitchen.

"Give me a second, Mom. I'm on my way in there. I can't hear you." Dez returned, walking toward the kitchen.

"Of course, you can't hear me. You have that phone in your ear," she said, noticing it as Dez walked in.

"Sorry about that," she giggled. "I see you picked up dinner. Who are you feeding? There's no way we'll be able to eat all of this food."

"I was hoping my boy was coming for dinner."

"You're boy, Mom? Now, Xavier is your 'boy'?"

"He's always been."

"You are so crazy. You know he's out on business. Well, that's the story he's sticking by," she teased.

"Don't you dare pick on my son-in-law, hurting his feelings." She took the phone out of Desirae's hands. "Hey, son-in-law, if she does anything, you be sure to let me know."

"Mom! Why would you do that?" Desirae grabbed the phone from her. "Do you mind if I call you back?" she fumed, disconnecting the call.

"We are *not* in a relationship, so why would you get on the phone calling him your son?" she blasted.

"He will be, and you know it. Now, calm down, Dez. You're overreacting."

"No, Mom, *you're* the one jumping the gun. That was out of line. I don't want him to get turned off because I'm showing too much interest or have you thinking that this is more than a friendship."

"Dez, if you don't go and call that man back . . . You're the only one living up to that 'friendship' title. That man sees you as way more than just a friend. You and I both know he wanted to take things slow because he met you at a session, and that was the best route to go. It didn't mean you'd stay and park there. Allow yourself to be happy and to experience real love, Dez. I'm sure your therapist tells you the same thing. Take the wall down and enjoy that man. You don't have to worry about him thinking you're perfect or have it all together. None of us do. Besides, look what he does for a living, and to top it off, he's a God-fearing man. You better get him before I do."

"Mom, I cannot talk to you anymore. You're nuts."

They erupted in laughter.

Swallowing her pride and fear, Desirae phoned Xavier back and apologized for overreacting. She let him know she didn't want him to think she was making more out of their friendship than what it was. Xavier didn't respond or react to her apology. He just asked if she would be available tomorrow evening because he'd be in town. Dez didn't know how to take him not entertaining the conversation and ending the call as quickly as he did.

Tomorrow could not have come fast enough. Before Desirae knew it, it was time to face the unknown. However, her nerves never had a chance to get the best of her because Dexter had called summoning everyone to the hospital for the arrival of Zayvon. Words could not begin to describe the emotional state Desirae was in seeing and holding her god-baby. She cried and fussed over him the entire time. For the first time in a long time, nothing else mattered to her. She'd been so busy trying to be a friend to Xavier without really confessing or showing her feelings unless they talked about it that she's been driving herself crazy. When in actuality, Desirae had fallen in love with Xavier awhile ago, and that's what scared her. Other than God, Xavier was the first and only man that she's grown to love.

As Dez and Rosalind left the hospital, her stomach did somersaults because it recognized after dropping Rosalind off, she'd be face-to-face with Xavier. Rosalind picked up on Dez's distracted state of mind.

"Dez, what's going on? It's like a whole other person just came out of that hospital with me."

"It's nothing, Mom. I'm all right."

"Sweetheart, *I* am the person who gave birth to you. If anyone knows you better than yourself outside of the Lord, it would be me. Now, cut the mess and talk to me."

"I think I messed things up with Xavier. I've been sick to my stomach," she blurted.

"First, calm down before you have a panic attack. Second, remember this is all God's doing. That man ain't going nowhere. I can promise you that one."

"That's not true, and there's no way you can promise that, Mom. And sometimes, God can bring things to us, and we can mess it up too."

"If God brings you to it, trust me, He will bring you through it. He knows the result of all things you're just in the middle of it and possibly the starting point. What you need to do is pay attention to what you're thinking. If you limit your thinking, your life will follow suit. Listen, Dez, if you believe in your heart that Xavier is your Boaz and he has found you, it's okay to admit it regardless of what name you two gave your relationship almost a year ago. If you love that man, tell him and stop playing these games. He wouldn't be spending all of this time with you on the phone and traveling to see you if he didn't feel the same."

"Mom, that is not true. Not once has he ever asked me to come and visit him. Xavier always comes to see me. I have no idea if he is really who he says he is. Plus, after that whole thing yesterday with you taking my phone, we haven't spoken like we usually do."

"Can he be a gentleman and want to get to know your world first before pulling you into his? Had he done that, you'd be saying everything is about him. Let me ask you something. Did he ever say he didn't want you in North Carolina?"

"No, he never said that. He told me if I were to come down there, I would come back home a few pounds heavier because we won't be eating salads. Xavier said his grandma taught him how to burn in the kitchen."

"If you don't quit your mess, talking about you messed up . . . Girl, grab my bag out the backseat when you come inside." Rosalind shook her head, exiting the car.

Rosalind and Naomi-Ruth have always been able to get Desirae back on track when she overthinks. However, this last intervention with Rosalind didn't last very long. This was the first time in a long time that Desirae had felt like this. She checked her reflection in the mirror a thousand times before leaving the house, and nothing fit or looked right, resulting in her changing outfits a million and one times—only to put back on the original outfit she'd planned to wear.

All the way to the restaurant, Dez kept thinking about turning around and going back to the house. Xavier had asked her to meet him at Antonino's Italian Restaurant because he loved pasta. However, it had her on edge. Anytime he'd come to town, Xavier picked Desirae up, and they'd go from there, which was another reason why she felt he was having her meet up with him to let her down easy.

"Hey, Xavier," she greeted him at the entrance.

"Hey, there, my friend." They embraced.

"Are you ready to go inside?" Desirae broke the embrace.

"Sure thing." He opened the door.

As the hostess led them to the table, Desirae considered telling Xavier she had a sudden emergency and needed to reschedule. However, she declined her mind's offer and took a seat instead.

"So, how was your day? How's Naomi-Ruth doing? What did she have?" Xavier asked.

"Oh my God, she's doing great, and Zayvon . . . He is beautiful. He's so precious I just want to eat him alive. I apologize for being late, but my godson made an early entrance."

"It's perfectly fine. This place doesn't close until 2:00 a.m. The lady told me that when I called."

"This place opens around three in the afternoon. I think that's why they have such late hours."

"Yeah, that's what I was told. So, do you want to have kids someday? I'm asking because you seem so excited over your godson."

"Shouldn't I be?"

"Of course. I guess I just wanted to know because I don't recall us ever talking about it before."

"After going through Nomi's pregnancy with her and seeing Zayvon for the first time, I'd love to experience motherhood for myself when God sends the right man my way."

"Sometimes, what God has for us could be sitting in front of us at Antonino's, but we are too blind to see it."

"Xavier, I know God sent you to show me there are good men out there—"

"I don't mean to cut you off, but before you continue, I've been meaning to ask you something, which is the reason why I invited you out. Can you fill this out for me, please?" He pulled a folded piece of paper out of his pocket.

"Fill something out?"

"Please, just open it."

Desirae opened the paper, and tears masked her face as she read:

> *Dear Desirae,*
> *Will you please be my girlfriend? I like you a lot.*
> *Please circle your answer: yes, no, or maybe.*
> *Xavier*

"Yes, yes, I would love to be your girlfriend," she blubbered.

Chapter Twenty-two

The Wages of Sin . . .

Dexter didn't think he could love anyone as much as he did his Ruth. But seeing Zayvon for the first time, he fell instantly in love the same way he did seeing Naomi-Ruth for the first time outside of his dreams. Since his son's birth, Dexter had asked the same question over and over. "Did my wife really just give birth to our son, or was it a dream?" Dexter's life was complete. God had blessed Pastor Lewis with a helpmeet and heir. It had been fifteen hours since Zayvon made his appearance into the world, and all that Dexter could think about was taking his family home. He and Naomi-Ruth were watching Zayvon as he slept after his feeding.

"Good morning, Mr. and Mrs. Patterson. I'm going to perform a hearing test on this little guy. The test isn't painful or invasive at all. It'll take only a few seconds top," Nurse Tosha from the neonatal unit informed them.

After several minutes passed, Dexter became impatient. "That's a long few seconds, don't you think, Nurse?"

"I apologize, but I had to run a second test. No worries, though. I will have the doctor come in and speak to you in a few minutes."

"Is there something wrong?" Naomi-Ruth raised concern.

"Let me have Dr. Boone come in. Zayvon didn't pass his screening, but I'm confident this is because he has a little fluid in his ears." She turned to exit the room.

"Don't be alarmed, Ruth. He's fine. It's probably the fluid, just like she just said."

At the conclusion of Dexter's sentence, Dr. Boone and Tosha returned. The doctor pretty much repeated what Tosha said. He also added that tomorrow, before they left the hospital to go home, they would retest him.

After the doctor confirmed the hearing test results, Dexter became a little uncomfortable. Zayvon wasn't born in sin but in marriage. God honors marriage. Therefore, it had to be the fluid, he told himself.

"Ruth, the devil is a liar. This is God's gift to us. He doesn't make mistakes, so there's no need for you to be crying. Pray. Better yet, I will."

Laying his hand on Zayvon's, Dexter petitioned God. "Dear Lord, we come to you today presenting our son, the child you blessed us with. We know you love us, and you can feel the tears we cry. You are the Master Healer. You said life and death are in the power of our tongue, so I speak against the test results about any form of hearing loss. The devil is a liar, and by Jesus' stripes, Zayvon is healed, and we count it done. In Jesus' name. Amen."

"Amen," Naomi-Ruth sniffled.

"Ruth, it's already done. All power is in God's hands, not the doctor's or a test. He gave us a perfectly healthy baby boy to love and grow with."

Less than twenty-four hours later, the doctor retested Zayvon, and again, he failed. The doctor suggested the hearing loss could be due to various scenarios. However, to determine the cause and the impact, he referred Zayvon to a pediatric audiologist for diagnostic testing.

"No no no, this has to be an error. God, we were right in your eyes. They're wrong. Ruth, they are wrong. Zayvon doesn't need any further tests. He can hear us. Look at him. There's nothing wrong with him. He's perfect." Dexter was unnerved.

"I believe God has it all in His hands, Dexter. I lay awake all night and prayed. Although my heart is aching, I believe God is a healer. No matter what, I will love Zayvon. He is perfect, regardless of what the test does or doesn't say."

Dexter's mind left the hospital room and hadn't returned, making him unable to respond to Naomi-Ruth.

The entire ride from the hospital was a silent one. Naomi-Ruth sat in the back, staring at her newborn, weeping about the unknown. Different scenarios, reasons, and recollections danced around Dexter's mind. Nothing was making sense to Pastor Lewis. God's greatness dismantled mistakes. We were all created in His likeness. How could this even be a topic of conversation or concern?

"This isn't God's work." Dexter slammed the car door behind him.

"Dexter, you have to calm down. You're going to frighten him."

"How, Ruth? How?"

"What kind of person are you? That's awful. We haven't even taken him to see the audiologist, and you're already acting this way." She lifted Zayvon from his car seat and cradled him.

Once inside, Dexter stormed off to the bedroom and slammed the door behind him again. Ruth didn't bother reacting to his outburst this time. All she desired was to sit in the rocking chair in the nursery and love on Zayvon. While in the bedroom, Dexter called G-ma Dye to let her know he'd be coming by for a visit. After finishing his call, he left the house without saying a word to Naomi-Ruth or acknowledging Zayvon.

Heading to his former condo where G-ma Dye now lived, Dexter drove at a high speed. The further he pondered, the harder he pushed the gas pedal.

"I picked up the distress in your voice over the phone. Is everything all right?" Dye rattled off as soon as she opened the door.

Gusting past her, Dexter paced back and forth, shaking his head, saying, "This can't be of God. There's no way."

"What are you talking about, Dex? What isn't of God? Better yet, where are Ruth and that precious little boy? Why aren't you home enjoying them? Didn't you just bring them home from the hospital?"

"I did, but something isn't right. God doesn't make mistakes, G-ma. We married before we had him, so how could he be born with a disability?"

"A disability? Slow down, son. What are you talking about?"

"Zayvon failed both of the hearing screenings. There's a possibility he won't be able to hear, I believe. The doctors at the hospital referred us to a specialist who will do further testing to see what's going on."

"In nothing that you just said did I hear he is deaf or that it's over. So, what's the problem? And please stop saying God doesn't make mistakes. That has nothing to do with any of this. You really should be with your wife. She needs you. Don't you think not knowing what's going on with Zayvon is hard on her too?"

"It would undoubtedly be hard on her if she were the reason for this to happen. Tamariane lost the baby because of sin, so that means Zayvon is going through this because of sin, and we know it's holiness and not hell for me."

"You sound foolish, Dexter. Sin has nothing to do with any of this, and your wife caused nothing. Maybe you should talk to someone because every time something happens, you cannot blame it on sin and continue comparing everything to what you experienced as a child, son."

"I talk to God every day, G-ma. I need not speak to anyone else. The bottom line is the wages of sin is death. My first child died because of sin. Our iniquities separate us from God. He hides His face from us because of our sins, and now, He won't hear us, and neither will Zayvon because of Ruth's sins."

"You don't sound right, son. You may *really* need to see someone. Better yet, committed for talking that foolishness. Romans six twenty-three says the wages of sin is death, but all that other stuff you added is not of or from God. The only person who needs to repent is you, Dexter. Just like Satan, pride comes before a fall, and I'm afraid for you. But you have to go through it so God can deliver you and bring you out of it."

"Repent? Sin cannot dwell in the presence of God, and I live in His presence."

"You're walking on dangerous grounds, Dexter. Watch what you say. The Bible instructs you as a leader to keep watch on everything you say and do. There's no way in the world you live in the presence of the God that I serve. My God is love, and what you are doing and saying isn't love or God, son. Stop and think about everything that has been going on. Remember, the church is as strong as our families are, and if your life is falling apart, so will the house of God. Look how many people left because of how you go off in a fit, beating the people of God with His words, which is the same thing you do to your wife."

Pastor Lewis disregarded Diane's rebuke, kissed her on the cheek, and made his way back home. G-ma Dye had always had a soft spot for Ruth. She wouldn't see what's standing in front of her, Dexter thought. He didn't agree with anything she'd said to him and believed her denial in all that he's said is a confirmation that Naomi-Ruth was the cause of the test results.

Chapter Twenty-three

Enough Is Enough . . .

The gentle motion of the chair should have comforted her, but the ache in her heart for her son wouldn't allow peace to come. Through her tears, she talked to her Heavenly Father, asking for strength. No matter what Dexter said, she knew when the results came back, what they would say. Naomi-Ruth's emotions hit her like an uncontrolled train at maximum velocity. She cried and cried more because she didn't want Zayvon to hurt or endure people's ignorance. Cradling him tighter, Naomi-Ruth cried herself to sleep after vowing that it was her job to protect Zayvon, and it is what she planned to do.

Ten days later, Desirae, Rosalind, and G-ma Dye accompanied Naomi-Ruth and Zayvon to the Children's Hospital for his appointment with the audiology department for his testing. Dexter had declined to attend. He has been distant since learning Zayvon had failed the initial screenings after he was born. Naomi-Ruth refused to allow his behavior to add any more pressure or stress. She buried herself in caring for her son. Every night, Naomi-Ruth would fall asleep in Zayvon's nursery. Dexter's whereabouts didn't matter. She pretended he wasn't there. Deep down inside, her heart pained because she wanted her husband to be involved and to continue loving their son as he had when he was first born. Zayvon was still perfect in Naomi-Ruth's eyes. She avoided Dexter because she knew he would end up saying something that would cause her even more pain.

After a course of analyses and a very intensive auditory brainstem response, they diagnosed Zayvon with acute sensorineural hearing loss. The medical team confirmed what Naomi-Ruth's heart had already told her. This type of hearing loss developed when there was a complication with the way the inner ear and the nerve work. It could result when there's destruction to the cells in the inner ear. This kind of hearing damage is generally permanent.

Naomi-Ruth smiled at her baby boy. She couldn't be weak, because now was the time to walk in her faith. Zayvon needed her, so Naomi-Ruth took in the air around her as she pushed Zayvon in his stroller and headed to break the news to the ladies in the lobby.

"Hey." Her lips trembled.

"No matter what it is, God is able," G-ma Dye assured her.

"What did they say?" Desirae sniffled.

"Well, my boy may not ever be able to hear what my voice sounds like. The test confirmed he has severe sensorineural hearing loss, and it could be genetic."

"God is still able, no matter what, Nomi." Dez wrapped her arms around her neck.

"I know He is. I just have to realize my experience as a first-time mom is going to be a little different than what I thought it'd be, and I'm okay with that. I will love Zayvon just the same."

"We all will," Rosalind, Desirae, and G-ma Dye sang in unison.

It burned Naomi-Ruth that Dexter wasn't with her when she and their son needed him. No matter what he felt or how terrified he might have been, his presence was required. Zayvon was his son. Now wasn't the time to withdraw. Whatever they needed to get through, they had to use it. This was their "for better or for worse." By the grace of God, Naomi-Ruth said they would endure even in heartache.

Rosalind decided to host dinner at her and Desirae's place on Saturday and invited G-ma Dye and Naomi-Ruth. They all agreed as Naomi-Ruth and G-ma Dye got out of the car and headed into the house when they returned home from the doctor's visit. Naomi-Ruth noticed Dexter's car out front and was happy he was home so she could share with him what was going on with Zayvon.

"Dexter, you should have come to that appointment with us and not let Ruth have to deal with all of this alone."

"I already knew what they were going to say. I didn't need to be present to confirm he's deaf. This is *her* doing. She already said she lost one child because of what happened to her. Our son is probably suffering because of it. Better yet, she was in this house for over a month and ended up pregnant. Are we sure he is even *my* child? Whatever the answer is, Ruth's sin is the cause of all of this."

"How could you be so cruel and cold? When I shared with you about my rape, I would never have thought you'd throw it back in my face. You were the first and only man I have been with," her voice cracked.

Naomi-Ruth's therapist had encouraged her to share with Dexter that she'd been raped and lost her rapist's baby. Dexter wept alongside his wife and promised to show her that there were good men in this world, and God had given her him, her good man. Never in a million years would she have thought he'd use it against her.

"*Second* man, Ruth. I am the *second* man."

"Dexter, that's enough. I don't know what has gotten into you but shut your mouth right now. The devil is a liar. I will not stand here and allow you to speak to this woman, your *wife,* like that," G-ma Dye corrected him.

"It's all right, Mother Diane. I expected him to react in this cowardly way. By no means did I think he'd say those cruel things, but I am not surprised. I thank God Zayvon can't hear the things you've said. Right now, I wish I were unable to hear, so I would not have met or married you. There isn't anything about what you've said or done that leads me to believe God's involved. God is a God of love. I'm not sure what happened to you to turn you into the person you're becoming, but whatever it is, you need to deal with it. But you won't be doing it here. I want you out of my house. Get your stuff and get out. I will *not* remain under the same roof as you. No matter how much all of this hurts, you *cannot* be here."

"This is *our* house. I am *not* leaving, Ruth. God doesn't ordain divorce, and if I leave this house, it will lead to that, and it's *not* happening."

"After everything you've said, do you *really* think I'm going to allow you to stay here? This house is in *my* name. We never changed it. It was left to me before we married. Now, please, leave."

"You will regret what you're doing."

"You know what? You've taught me so much about love. A person can worship the ground that you walk on and could be the worst thing for you at the same time. Just because you love me doesn't mean you're for me. I will not become your lap dog and allow you to punish me or my son any longer. To think I forgave you because of your confession and tears. Just because a person cries doesn't mean they're sorry or they're going to change."

Pastor Lewis packed a few things and tearfully left with G-ma Dye back to his former home. Naomi-Ruth felt as if her whole world had caved in on her. Zayvon's diagnosis and splitting up with Dexter were the last things she could have imagined. She loved Dexter with everything in her, but she loved herself and Zayvon more.

Chapter Twenty-four

When It Rains, It Pours . . .

Desirae always had her reservations about Pastor Lewis from the time they appointed him the head pastor. She struggled with his controlling ways. His actions barely took her aback. However, the way he turned his back on Naomi-Ruth and Zayvon blew her mind. When Nomi phoned her after Dexter left, Dez shed tears all the way back over to Naomi-Ruth's house.

"Nomi, are you all right? I know this is probably the hardest thing you've ever had to endure outside burying your parents. No matter what, you know I am here with you and my godson through it all."

"I feel so empty inside, Dez. He went from husband and then father of the decade to accusing me of sleeping with someone else and has abandoned his son and me. Had he stayed, he would not have been present. Dexter hardly said two words to me after we brought Zayvon home. He blames me, Dez." She broke down.

"Something is missing in all of this. He seems so unstable, Nomi. If I learned anything in therapy and from talking to Xavier, Pastor Lewis deflects. It bothers me so much that he uses the Bible to throw everything and everyone off course. He criticizes and blames everyone for everything. I think something happened to him, and he has his own skeletons. That's why he is the way that he is."

"Dez, I'm not sure of anything right now. I can't even deal with the hurt from not being able to do anything to make things better for my son because I have to have a shouting match with my husband. He was so mean, Dez."

"Right now, our primary concern is Zayvon. Let God deal with Pastor Lewis. I know it pains you, but right now, you don't have any other choice."

After shedding tears with her friend, Desirae allowed Naomi-Ruth to get herself and Zayvon settled and later headed back home. While on the road, she called Xavier for some words of comfort. All of what was going on with Nomi was a hard pill for her to swallow. Dez was trying her best to take in Nomi's pain and be strong for her, but she felt she was hurting as much as Naomi-Ruth. Even though Dez believed Naomi-Ruth and Pastor Lewis rushed into marriage, she admired their union in the same breath. When Pastor Lewis was Dexter, as Naomi-Ruth would say, when he wasn't in his clergy collar, he showered Nomi with a love that Dez prayed she'd receive someday. The man that he turned into once he picked up the Bible was someone Desirae didn't agree with or like.

"Hey, Xavier, did I catch you at a bad time?"

"Not at all, beautiful. What's troubling you? I can hear the sadness in your voice."

"So much is going on . . . I don't even know where to begin. Forgive me for crying in your ear, but I just hate that Nomi is dealing with all of this at the same time."

"Desirae, I don't want you ever to feel the need to apologize for showing emotion. If you have to cry, let it out. Now, tell me what's going on."

"Remember, I told you Zayvon failed his hearing test at the hospital before being discharged?"

"Yes, I do, and you said the doctors said it might not have meant anything, right?"

"Correct. However, we went with Nomi today to take him for more testing, and they said he has some genetic thing. I can't remember the name of it, and that he's deaf. That breaks my heart into a million pieces, especially when Nomi said her son wouldn't ever hear her voice. All of this is a lot to deal with at once. I feel like I can't breathe right now."

"Take a deep breath, Dez. Just breathe and talk to me. Talking will help you avoid having a panic attack. Let me ask you a question. How's Pastor Lewis dealing with all of this?"

"I didn't even get to him. He blamed Nomi for it. He even used her being raped against her. It's like he wants nothing to do with Zayvon. He said sin caused him to be deaf, and not just any sin—Nomi's sins. He accused her of possibly cheating."

"Now, I see why you had an emotional breakdown. What I need you to do is remember, none of this can be fixed or changed overnight, and guess what?"

"What?"

"You will not have the answers to it all. You will get confused at times, and it will be painful, but God has you and Naomi-Ruth here, so He will bring you through it. I'm so sorry Pastor Lewis reacted in the way that he did, but in my professional opinion, this is deeper than what's on the surface. He's hurting, and the only way hurt individuals know how to deal with it is to hurt other people."

"It's so funny you say that because I just told Nomi the same thing."

"Pray for him and allow them to work that part out. They're married. Naomi-Ruth will do what's best for her and her family. You might end up not agreeing with her decision, but just be there for her no matter what."

"I have been from day one. Pastor Lewis proposed and prepared a wedding ceremony down to picking out Nomi's dress."

"I don't understand. What're you saying?"

"Pastor proposed during service and sent Nomi downstairs to put on her dress while they fixed the church up for them to get married. He even wrote their vows."

"That's a lot. We have to pray and let this play out the way that it's supposed to. Right now, the baby is the priority. Getting him the help he needs outweighs everything else. Naomi-Ruth will need you because this will be a trying season, but there's nothing too hard for God."

"I love talking to you. I feel like a weight has been lifted. I just pulled up to my place. I'll call you a little later, all right?"

"Sure thing, beautiful. I'll be waiting."

As Desirae reached the door, the smell of burnt food greeted her, along with smoke, when she opened the door. The smoke detector was screaming in the background as she called out for Rosalind.

"Ma!" Dez yelled when she opened the door.

There was no answer, so she headed toward the kitchen. As she got closer, a faint, charred smell invaded her nostrils.

"Ma!" she repeated.

"Nooooo!" she yelled as she stepped to the door and saw Rosalind on the floor with blood on her head.

The back door had been kicked in, and a chair was turned over, and the table was pushed out of place. All that registered in a split second as she rushed to where Rosalind was sprawled on the floor.

Apparently, Rosalind was at the stove, cooking greens, and someone broke in through the back door and assaulted her. They took all of their jewelry and cash that was in the house. Rosalind's purse and both of their laptops were stolen, as well. The assailant had left her in a pool of blood. The ambulance rushed Rosalind to the hospital where she was pronounced dead from blunt force trauma. Someone had violently hit her on the head with an object, and that blow took her life.

It had been four days since Rosalind's death, and Desirae hadn't said a word. She refused to eat. All she did was sit inside their home and cry. Xavier had been in town since the night of the break-in.

Before finding out about the murder, Naomi-Ruth didn't want to sit in the house alone, so she packed Zayvon's and her things into an overnight bag and headed to Rosalind and Desirae's. She knew they wouldn't have a problem with them being there. However, when she arrived, she was met by flashing lights. Getting out of the car, she could see police officers and the paramedics by Desirae's door. Strapping Zayvon to the front of her, Naomi-Ruth ran toward all the commotion. When she got closer to the door, she saw Desirae on her knees, crying and screaming at the top of her lungs with bloodstains on her shirt, hands, and face.

"Dez, are you all right? What happened to you?"

"Nomi, someone hurt Mom and robbed us. She wasn't breathing. I tried to help her."

"No, nooooo. This is not happening," Naomi-Ruth *cried out, cradling Zayvon.*

Naomi-Ruth refused to leave Desirae's side even though she didn't feel comfortable having Zayvon in the emergency room with her. She waited in the lobby and took Dez's phone while she was out there and phoned Xavier to let him know what had happened. While she was on the phone with him, she was informed that Rosalind had passed away. Xavier was in New Jersey on business. After talking to Naomi-Ruth, he cancelled his lecture and took a taxi to New York, Long Island, to be exact. The cost didn't matter. All Xavier wanted was to be by Desirae's side during her time of need.

The service was scheduled for today, and although things between Naomi-Ruth and Dexter had been rocky, they put aside their differences to make the arrangements for Rosalind's funeral. Despite Pastor Lewis's ways, Rosalind loved and respected her pastor. She would tell Desirae it would only be a matter of time before God cut Pastor down to size and humbled him really good. Dez would shake her head and wished it happened sooner than later for Nomi's sake. In any event, Pastor Lewis was at the podium, preparing to begin officiating the service as Rosalind would have desired.

"We are gathered here today to seek and to receive comfort. I would be lying if I said our hearts aren't aching over the loss of our beloved sister, Rosalind Cooke. God, we come here today, asking for you to minister to our hearts and Sister Desirae's heart. Give her strength, Heavenly Father. We thank you in advance for wrapping your arms around the bereaved family, dear Lord.

"You know if Sister Rosalind were able to say something right now, she'd say, 'Let the Lord use you, Pastor. We need a Word.'"

"Amen. Yes, she would. She loved the Word," the mourners chimed in.

"Our circumstances in life can alter without notice, and at times, worsen. In those dark times, we should draw closer to God. He is the source of our strength. In Him is where we have to seek refuge. Our natural man might be tempted to become bitter in these times, but that won't change things. Only God can carry us through the valley experiences. We cannot allow ourselves to operate in our flesh. Anything that's a result of the flesh cannot be an heir of God's promise. The story of Ishmael in the Bible teaches us to wait on God because when we act on impulse taking matters into our own hands, kicking our husbands out of our homes, backbiting, murmuring, and complaining, we're operating out of our flesh. Sometimes, you can't move forward until you recognize where you've failed. Sickness and ailments are liable to attach themselves to you and your children when you disobey God. And you will end up just like Hagar, the bondwoman, and a child of a bondwoman cannot be an heir."

"You are a sick man! How could you get up there at my mother's funeral and say those things? What is *wrong* with you?" Desirae exploded before running out of the church with Xavier on her heels.

Naomi-Ruth cried as she raced out the door behind Xavier and Desirae.

Chapter Twenty-five

Lord, I Trust You . . .

Rosalind's service was the last place Naomi-Ruth had expected Dexter to act out in the way that he had. He humiliated her in the worst way possible. Not only that, he made a difficult, heart-wrenching time even more tragic. Disgust, anger, embarrassment, and regret plagued Naomi-Ruth's soul because of her association with Dexter. She was sad for his soul. He had to be a troubled man without a heart to stand in front of the church at a funeral and say the things that he said.

Naomi-Ruth did her best to console Desirae, but it was almost impossible. They couldn't get a word in because they'd break down in tears just looking at each other. Desirae felt remorseful for Naomi-Ruth and vice versa. Dez has been staying with Naomi-Ruth since Rosalind's murder, and Xavier has been right by her side. Naomi-Ruth was happy to have them there.

In the midst of everything that had been going on, she had been battling with the fear of raising her son alone—her deaf son. He had an appointment today to receive his first hearing aids. Naomi-Ruth hadn't had time to review the literature she received or make the appointments she needed to make because she'd been mourning the loss of Rosalind and Dexter. To her, it's as if he passed away at the funeral. There was no way in the world he could love her and denounce her and Zayvon in front of their church family and friends. Part of her wished she would have listened to Dez when they were downstairs before the wedding. Then the other part of her was grateful because had she not married Dexter, Zayvon wouldn't be here. Naomi-Ruth loved her son. She talked to him and treated him as if he heard and understood everything she said.

What Naomi-Ruth feared most was how people would stare and treat Zayvon when they saw the hearing aid in his ears. She didn't want her son to be treated as if he were abnormal. Xavier helped her calm down after a talk they'd had. He'd walked past the nursery and overheard Naomi-Ruth crying, talking to Zayvon.

"I love you, Zay. I know you can't hear me, but you will learn to read my lips one day. I wish you could hear my voice so that you would know everything is going to be all right."

"He knows, Naomi-Ruth. That boy is comfortable and content, staring back at you."

Xavier startled her.

"I didn't even hear you come in. Do you think he really knows everything will be all right?"

"Of course, he does. There isn't anything different going on between the two of you right now than it would be for a hearing child. You are giving him the same love, attention, care, mother-son relationship that any new mom would give her newborn. The only difference will be how you will communicate with each other later on down the line. Right now, all he needs is what you're giving him . . . love."

"Thank you so much, Xavier. I didn't even give myself a chance to look at it that way, but you're absolutely right. And thank you for being what my Dez needs right now."

"You don't have to thank me. God knows what He's doing even when everything looks like it's falling apart. These light afflictions are only for a moment. Think about all of the things that God has already brought you through. If He did it before, He will do it again. Pray for your husband and learn to forgive him. I am not saying you have to take him back or anything like that. That's between you, him, and God. What I *am* saying is don't allow that stuff to fester on your heart for too long. It'll be hard to get it off. You have too much love sitting in your arms to have any offense in your heart."

Xavier's words resonated in Naomi-Ruth's heart. Although things hadn't changed, she felt good about the possibility of change and accepting things for what they were. His words were what she was carrying with her to Zayvon's appointment, along with trusting that God hadn't given her the spirit of fear.

Because the funeral was two days ago, Naomi-Ruth didn't bother asking Dez to accompany her and Zay. She also wanted to get comfortable with Zay having equipment for his ears before dealing with anyone else's questions or sympathy. The last thing Naomi-Ruth wanted was for anyone to feel sorry for her or Zayvon.

The hour that Naomi-Ruth had anxiously dreaded was here. Questions of . . . If Zayvon was deaf, why did he need hearing aids, and other unknowns had tormented her, causing nervous shakes. She felt nauseated sitting in the waiting room for the five minutes that she'd been there.

Maybe I should reschedule and come back after I've read over the material I received at his last appointment, she pondered.

Before Naomi-Ruth could follow through her thoughts, she and Zayvon were brought into the exam room, where the audiology team awaited them.

"Good morning, Mrs. Lewis. Before we begin, I want to put you at ease and answer all the questions you have," the audiologist, Harry, said comfortingly.

"Well, first, I would like to know why Zayvon would require hearing aids when he was diagnosed as being deaf. If I am not mistaken, that means he's unable to hear, correct?"

"Sensorineural hearing loss is a form of hearing loss, and there's a strong chance that it can be managed with hearing aids. The hearing aids will alert Zayvon by providing a sense of sound to give him a higher awareness of everything around him."

"How will I know they're working?"

"We will routinely conduct additional testing to monitor his progress."

"I apologize for asking a million questions, but Zayvon is the first deaf person that I have ever met. And he's my child. I don't want him to suffer."

"This is a new experience. Like learning a new job, everything seems foreign, but over time, you adjust—the same with hearing aids. Zayvon will adjust, and so will you. He will not suffer. He can still have a normal life, obtain a good education, job, and everything else."

"Thank you so much, Harry. I have been overthinking when I know better."

"It's perfectly fine and normal."

Naomi-Ruth left the audiologist's office more at ease. Her primary concern now is that she is responsible for maintaining the hearing aids. The audiology team was excellent and made her feel comfortable with everything while there. They just wouldn't be at her side while at home, which frightened her. Harry and his team reassured her that they'd be there every step of the way. The volume of information they gave her was what overwhelmed her and had her terrified. But to know

Zayvon had a support system in place calmed some of her anxiety.

After getting Zayvon settled and his car seat strapped into the car, Naomi-Ruth climbed in and sat next to him, and through a thunderstorm of tears, she petitioned her Heavenly Father.

"Father, I don't understand, and I don't know why, but I do know whatever is spiraling around my life right now, you are my perfect peace. I know that you are working it all together for my good. God, I need you right now to help me keep my eyes and focus on you and not the circumstances surrounding my marriage or Zayvon. Please, God, stay by his side. Send angels to encamp around my baby. I am thanking you in advance for your comfort and healing power. I know what the doctors said, but I also know what you said. I speak healing over my child, no matter what my eyes see or what people say. In the midst of it all, I trust you, even though the pain in my life makes you seem so far away. No matter what, God, I know you're able to do exceedingly abundantly above all that I can ask or think. The glory belongs to you, God. Please, heal Zayvon."

Finishing her plea to the Lord, Naomi Ruth looked down at her sleeping son and broke down.

Chapter Twenty-six

The Troubles of the Past . . .

After Desirae and Naomi-Ruth walked out of the church during Rosalind's going home service, the attendees followed suit, different groups at a time. Before leaving, Xavier advised the funeral director that Desirae would come by the parlor to pay her final respects the following day. All this, while Pastor Lewis continued with his sermon.

"When we run from the truth, it will chase us down."

In the middle of him speaking, the sound system stopped working, and his microphone cut off. Looking around and shaking his mic, Pastor Lewis looked confused because he was so caught up in getting his message out that he hadn't noticed everyone pretty much walked out. He heard Desirae's response but ignored it and kept speaking. Since he ministered with his eyes closed and tuned everything out so he could deliver the Word he felt God gave him for the mourners, he missed that most of them had left, even Naomi Ruth. As his eyes jumped around, Pastor Lewis's nerves got the best of him. When he realized that he, Mother Diane, and only a few of the other church mothers were the only persons left, it caused his proud frame to slump and Mother Diane to intervene.

"Forgive me, Mothers, but I have to deal with this once and for all," G-ma Dye apologized.

"Dye, it's been long overdue. Do what God has been telling you to do. And, Pastor, remember these words this very day: The crash is here because of your pride. Your ego made the fall that you're going through, and that same ego will make what you're about to go through even harder. But God *will* get the glory. Let all of that stuff go, son. It has had you bound long enough. God has great works for you, but you're in your own way. Let it go, son," Mother Celine declared, making her way to the door.

The remaining two church mothers followed Mother Celine's lead, leaving Mother Dye alone with Pastor. As the mortician and company prepared Rosalind's remains to be transferred back over to the funeral parlor, Pastor Lewis and G-ma Dye confronted each other for the first time. They both knew it was time to expose the suppressed truths that had led to the pain that had weighed them down through the years.

"Dexter, your actions have aroused the anger of God, and you've brought everything that is happening on yourself. Although I am partly responsible for your secret suffering, I had to cut the sound system off. How dare you get up there and say those things?"

"Mother Diane, I gave God's people what He gave me, and what do you mean you caused me pain?"

"Right now, this is your grandmother talking to you. All of these titles, agendas, doctrines, and everything else are what have you in a spiritual state of delusion. This is a sign that Jesus will be coming back soon, and, Dexter, you and I both have to get things right so that we aren't left behind."

"I rebuke that statement. I have never taken delight in betraying God or rejecting Him. How dare you say that I am in a state of delusion."

"You know the truth, Dexter, but your arrogant disdain has your mind warped. There are some things that I haven't been straightforward with you about, and I believe it has led to further injury," she choked out.

"I am not injured, G-ma. Would you please stop saying that. You didn't cause anything. Sin is the reason for anything that happens out of the will of God."

"You might have a point because I wasn't honest with you about why my girls no longer speak to you or me. How can you preside over a church when our household is so messed up?"

When Ramona, Taniece, Chanté, and Alethea learned Dexter had impregnated a young woman from the church, they were in shock. They'd presumed he didn't have any interest in girls. When they were around him, they teased him, saying, "Little Miss CinderFella done lifted his dress and turned into a man." Ramona particularly tormented him the most. It wasn't until she heard about the demise of Dexter and Tamariane's baby that she felt the need to unleash all of her pent-up resentment. Sunday dinner hadn't been the same since.

"I'm sorry to hear about your little one, Dex," Ramona sneered.

"If you're sorry, why are you smirking? But thank you . . . I guess."

"Because I'm not surprised this happened. Every time you're attached to a pregnant woman, a tragedy happens. Ultimately, someone dies."

"Stop it, Ramona. Shut your mouth. How dare you come in here talking this foolishness," G-ma Dye reprimanded.

"Why, Momma Dee? All of the church and preaching y'all do, God told none of you to tell the truth? You and Pop Reg act like she never existed. Everyone bows down to Dexter when he is the reason my sister is dead."

Ramona never saw it coming. The sharp sting of Momma Dee's palm to her face stopped her rant mid-sentence.

Grabbing her face, Ramona screamed, "That's what your God taught you to do? Hit your children for telling the truth? I thought you said the truth would set us free. How can you be free when that little boy you always protecting is the reason my sister is dead?"

"Get out of my house. I will not tolerate disrespect. Until you learn how to show love and respect to every member of this family, you're not welcomed here."

"Dye, that's harsh," Pop Reg interjected.

"Reg, if there was ever a time you needed to be by my side and support my decision, this is that time," Momma Dee sniffled.

Ramona, Taniece, Chanté, and Alethea glanced at one another through tearstained eyes, and without having to say a word, they got up from the table at the same time. They gathered their kids up to leave.

"You don't have to worry about us. God will take care of us better than you or your nasty husband ever have," Ramona said, slamming the door.

"What is she talking about, G-ma," Dexter whined.

"Nothing, baby. Your sister is still hurting because of your mother's passing. All of us are. It's just taking

*the girls longer to heal," G-ma Dye said, breaking
down.*

It had been years since Dexter or G-ma Dye spoke
to or had seen the girls. Dye has had a hole in her soul
because of the fallout. It had weighed heavily on her
heart, along with not admitting the truth and rectifying
things for her family. Telling the truth, in her mind,
would have caused more harm. Therefore, she shunned
away from Anastasia's pregnancy and death. However,
because of Dexter's behavior, Dye couldn't carry the
loaded truth any longer.

"Dexter, remember when Ramona said it was your fault
your mother, my baby girl, went home to be with the
Lord after giving birth to you?"

"Her words are engraved in my heart. I grieve daily
because I never got to know her, and she's gone so that I
can live. Sometimes, I have a hard time processing that
because I was created in sin. But the wages of sin are
death, so on the other hand, I understand."

"I need you to stop thinking like that and talk to someone. The love of God and His grace are immense. He
wants to take away our heartache and the consequences
of our sins. That's why Jesus died on the cross. He paid
the price, so we don't have to. But you have to understand that even though God allowed Jesus to perish for
our sins, death and suffering still exist. Sometimes, we
get caught up in things out of our control, and as a result,
we are crippled in many ways because of someone else's
actions. Your mother was a sweet little girl. Just like you,
at a young age, Anastasia found God. It wasn't her fault,
Dex. She was in the restroom at the church and taken

advantage of. Her 11-year-old body was mistreated and raped. She didn't ask for it to happen, and neither did God punish her for any of it, son. Some people are sick and need help, and if they don't get it, things that are lying dormant inside of them metastasize like cancer and kills them. Their judgment is off, and they hurt everyone in their path."

"What are you saying, G-ma?" Dexter cried.

"I-I am so sorry. I didn't know how to explain or even talk about this, because I feel as if it's all my fault."

"What, G-ma? What? Please, tell me."

"You're Pop Reg was sick. He messed up, but Bishop prayed, fasted, and counseled him, and Reg got himself together."

"Got himself together?"

"I love you, Dex. I never wanted to hurt you, but because of my guilt, I sheltered and tried to protect you. Doing so, I pushed the girls away. They had every reason to feel how they did toward Reg, but I made them love him and didn't talk to them. I just yelled at them and told them God would take care of it all, and we all fell short of the glory of God."

"Are you saying that Pop Reg hurt my mother, G-ma?"

Dexter squinted, staring out into the distance as if he were in a trance. Learning that he was a product of rape made his body spasm with no control over himself. Identical to a tonic-clonic convulsion, Dexter felt himself losing awareness, and as his muscles stiffened, he fell to the floor.

"My life is a lie. I've been living a lie. I am the son of a rapist. He verbally abused me every chance he had, G-ma. And he was my *father?* I've constantly wondered how my features resembled Pop Reg so much. My nose, mouth, and mannerisms mimicked his. I assumed it was because people say when you're around someone for a long period that you begin to look alike. Never would I have thought he was my mother's rapist. Maybe deep down inside, I knew. Maybe that's why I pushed my wife and son away. I am damaged goods. You know when we brought Zayvon home, it paralyzed me in fear, afraid that I'd hurt him. How could you let me go on living a lie, G-ma?" he grieved.

Pastor Lewis and G-ma spent the rest of the day and evening inside of the church crying and talking. Dexter was feeling broken and left to bleed. In fact, he knew now that he had been oozing out all over the place for a long time. He'd covered up all of the uncertainties, insecurities, and the pain of not knowing who he really was outside of his clergy collar.

"My hands have been dirty, and I've been mishandling God's people with my unresolved stuff, G-ma."

"There is a way of escape, Dex. God didn't bring us this far to leave us."

"I'll have to step down as pastor. I need time to heal from the surgery God is about to do in my life. I need some time alone with God. Do you think you could give me that?"

"We need to clear everything up. I don't want to leave without making sure you're all right. A lot was said, and I, again, Dex, I am truly sorry. All I ever wanted was to protect you. I took matters into my own hands and away from God and made things worse."

The words G-ma were saying made no impact. Dexter was lost in the aching misery of the revelation. Staring at his hands, he saw what no one else could see . . . dirt where there was none. In his devastated mind, the filth of a lifetime of sins was on his hands. He didn't want G-ma Dye or anyone to see him in his filthy state any longer.

"Right now, I can't even think straight. I need to start cleaning myself up. Please, give me a minute. I'll go back to the house, and we can finish talking later."

G-ma Dye made a tearful path to the exit, and Pastor Lewis locked the church up behind her. Unsure of where to go, who to turn to, or what to do, Dexter fell to his knees in the spot he stood, crying out to God in prayer.

"Dear Lord, this is your servant. I come to you with my arms stretched wide. I ask that you give me the strength to forgive. I kneel before you confused, angry, damaged, and feeling abandoned by the ones that were supposed to love me. I am afraid of who I could become learning where I came from. Be near me, dear God, in my hour of trouble. May your healing power rest upon me, cleansing, rebuilding, and giving me the strength to be anew. Please, grant your grace and mercy to help me let go and free myself of the things I've allowed to fester. Forgive me for getting ahead of your plans and for my pride. Help me to come to you for direction, provision, and protection as I deal with the things I've created. I need you, God. I can't do this without you."

Pastor Lewis spent the balance of the evening and the remainder of the week inside of the sanctuary. He lay prostrate before the Lord and wept in prayer from sunup until the sunlight faded from the sky. Unsure of where to turn or what to do because he knew he had to face the consequences of his actions, he penned letters to Desirae and the church council. He also wrote a separate note for his spouse. Dexter apologized to the heads of the church and apprised them of his choice to step down as pastor until he could see clearly and be the leader God called him to be. This was one of the toughest decisions for him to have to make, as it left him indeed further confused about what he should do or where to go.

"God, I am stepping down. I feel the tugging at my heart to do so, but what next? I don't know what else to do. There's no way I can recover right now, sitting in the face of it all. I am too fragile. I come to you as humble as I know how. Please show me what you want—"

From nowhere, the echo of his cell phone tore through the temple, causing him to jump in nervousness, cutting his prayer short. Without a second thought, Dexter grabbed the phone and answered it.

"H-hello, Pastor speaking."

"Good afternoon, Pastor Lewis. This is Pastor Xavier Washington, Sister Desirae's friend. I hope you don't mind me calling. Mother Diane gave me your number."

"No problem. How can I help you?"

"Is it possible for us to meet and talk? I'm by the church. I can meet you there."

"It'd be best if we spoke now, over the phone, if that's all right with you."

Pastor Lewis hadn't showered or shaved in days, and he wasn't up to seeing anyone, either. The best he could provide was a brief phone conversation, considering he thought he turned his ringer off.

"Speaking face-to-face would be easier, Pastor. I have been praying for you since the first day that we met. Every leader and person of good needs covering. You know, someone to talk to and be open and honest with, without the titles. Just you and me. Xavier and Dexter."

"Now isn't a good time."

"Pastor, I know you haven't left the church since the funeral service. I am standing outside. Please let me in. I had no intention of coming this way, but somehow, it was God's doing. Of course, I ran into Mother Diane. I stopped for gas, and she pulled up on the side of me said God told her to give me your number when she saw me. So, I am here, and I am not leaving, Pastor."

Everything inside of Dexter refused to open the door, but his body turned against him. Before he could even think about it, Pastor Lewis was unlocking the church doors to allow Xavier to enter.

"My brother, I feel in my heart God sent you here. I don't know what to do. This here shell of a man standing before you is messed up. You should probably leave before I rub off on you," Pastor Lewis confessed.

"Well, from the sound of things, I hear a man that is on the threshold of clearing up his mess."

"You would say that it's relatively biblical, but I need what you said on the phone. Dexter and Xavier. There can be no Pastor Lewis until Dexter is put back together."

"One thing about me is I don't say what people want to hear all of the time. The man that greeted and confessed to me is not the same person who was standing in that pulpit almost a week ago. You owned your stuff, and you were honest with me. As leaders and men of God, we need not hide our flaws. We have to stand in the face of our shortcomings, as you just did. When we are broken, we are humbled, and God can only use us in our humility. No one knows the pressure to be the idea of perfection more than us leaders, but we got it all wrong. We serve a perfect God, and because of our imperfections, Jesus died on the cross.

"Look, Dexter, there are some things you need to deal with. You cannot overcome them by masking them with religious work. To be an effective man and then a leader, we have to clear those things we hold on to and continue to trip over. You don't have to tell me anything, and I don't want you to because I can feel the pain that has had you captive for far too long. Some of that pain is old and some new, but it's deep, and if you don't get it under control, it will drive you crazy—or kill you. The Word is right all by itself, but God gave us tools to help us more with those other things. As leaders, we carry so much of our baggage and think by helping others that we are helping ourselves. After a while, if we continue to ignore those things gnawing at us, we infect the lives of the people we connect with and the ones connected to us.

"Pastor, I am not sure how you feel about this, but I think you need time to work on that inner man and talk to a faith-based counselor. Someone you don't know who can help you unload the baggage you've been carrying, along with the new baggage you've acquired."

"I was just asking God what's next, and you called," he broke down.

Dexter heard what Xavier was speaking, but his long-held belief kicked in. Handing it over to God should be sufficient. However, moments later, his life occurrences flashed before him, along with the things Xavier said, forcing Pastor Lewis to realize God was with him through it all, answering his prayer and sending Xavier to the church door. And after learning more about Restoration House, Dexter agreed to sign himself into the faith-based treatment center. Repairing himself was heavy on his mind. Restoration House offered Christian counseling services for the whole individual focusing on personal, emotional, and spiritual matters that we deal with daily, and Dexter desperately yearned for help. He didn't know where else to turn. Although he recognized he would neglect his responsibilities as pastor, husband, and father, he needed this time. And he also understood he was of no use to anyone if he wasn't good to himself. After adding to the letter he composed for Naomi-Ruth, Dexter had Xavier drive him to Restoration House in New Jersey.